Amethyst Awakening
The Gifted Reborn

by

T. H. Tracy

WWW.OAKLEAPRESS.COM

Amethyst Awakening: The Gifted Reborn © 2022 by T. H. Tracy. All rights reserved. No part of this book may be used or reproduced in any manner whatsoever without written permission except in the case of brief quotations embodied in critical articles and reviews. For information visit:

www.OakleaPress.com

Chapter 1

The world around him came into sharp focus. The field stretched as far as the eye could see—waving grains of gold. He looked down to see his feet sunk into the warm earth. It was daylight out, just after dawn. He closed his eyes and took in the smell. It was rich and bold, assaulting his senses and making him dizzy.

He quickly opened his eyes. He had no time for this. He had to find her. She could be anywhere. She always called him when he'd been asleep for hours, when he was the most vulnerable. After all this time, he still didn't know her name. She was still just The Girl to him.

He never fought the call. At first, he'd been confused. He'd thought it was a dream like anyone might have. He'd dreamed of a girl on a farm from old times or far away. She wore a long, dark green shift and had her dark hair in tresses down her back. She never said a word to him but beckoned him to follow. It might have been only a dream, except he saw her again a few nights later. She wore the same dress. Her hair was the same way. This time she gave him a sip of milk from a ladle out of a wooden bucket. It was cool and tasted frothy and thick.

He might have dismissed these nightly visits as products of his imagination if she hadn't continued to come. She never talked. He sometimes spoke to her, and she sometimes smiled, nodded, and gestured, but she never said a word. He began to wonder if they knew the same language, but she seemed to understand him.

Then again, if it was his dream, she probably would.

Seon was not particularly close to any of the kids at school. He'd often wished to have a best friend—someone he could confide in on a day-to-day basis. This would be the time he would tell his friend about the girl he visited in his dreams and his need to find her. It was beyond a necessity at this point. It was turning into an obsession, since he didn't know her name. He could barely describe her face; it always seemed washed out in the dreams, but he knew somehow that she was real.

She was real, and she needed his help.

Although he didn't have any friends he was close to, Seon could imagine what one would say at this point. How do you know she is a real person and not just a figment of your imagination? What makes you think she is communicating with you? How can you visit this girl in your dreams? Is it teleporting? Astral-projection? If you are traveling hundreds or maybe thousands of miles to another land in your sleep, wouldn't you know it?

In these hypothetical conversations, Seon always felt that although he didn't know the answers, it didn't change the fact that The Girl was still out there, trying to communicate with him. Somehow, she succeeded, and Seon found himself in that field, standing with her. Whether he physically left his bed or not didn't matter. He was there with her one way or another.

And so, he started drawing. Seon's notebooks had previously been filled with nothing but plants. Soon, pictures of the mysterious girl popped up alongside the drawings of orchids and wheat hybrids, and eventually, there were more sketches of her than there were of plants. Eventually, his notebooks were filled with images of her, just as his head was consumed with visions of her.

Who she was and what she wanted became less and less

important. All that mattered was how to find her. The other kids in the class didn't notice Seon staring into space because that was mostly what he did anyway. The only classes he ever paid any attention to were science classes. Even then, he never spoke to anyone unless it was group work or an assigned task. Talking to girls made him nervous and giddy. He'd nearly stabbed Chloe Primrose with the scalpel during their last botany lab because he'd been shaking so much.

With *her*, it was so much different, and she might not even be real? Impossible. She had to be real, and he would find her.

Chapter 2

The cafeteria was buzzing with activity and noise, just like always. Seon hated it. He didn't mind other kids and often wanted to be around them. He just preferred them in small doses. He would have liked to walk up to a group, sit down, and join in the conversation, but that desire was more theoretical. He could never see himself ever doing it. He preferred to stick to himself and think that he might do that another day.

For now, Seon walked across the room and avoided the raucous shouts of his classmates, none of which were directed at him. As usual, he blended in without really trying. That was easy when he was medium-height and build with mouse-colored hair and skin the color of dark sawdust and black, close-cropped hair. When he got to the sandwich vendor, he glared at the brightly colored display of perfect, delicious-looking sandwiches that would be nothing like what was inside. It seemed pointless to choose because, to Seon, they also had the same tasteless blandness. He jabbed his finger at the peanut butter sandwich with a sigh, wondering if it would contain anything resembling peanut butter.

When he reached down to take the plastic-wrapped package out of the tray at the bottom of the machine, someone else grabbed it instead. Seon stood up quickly in surprise, raising his eyebrows at the sandwich thief. He was more confused than alarmed.

"Are you really going to eat this?" Seon's thief held the package up with two fingers in over-exaggerated disgust. "I'm not sure that a hazmat crew shouldn't come to take it away."

"Food is food," Seon said mildly, taking the sandwich back.

This type of incident was not uncommon in most high schools, so Seon was ready to dismiss it as typical roughhousing. The other kid, a boy he thought was named Aron, hadn't been overly vicious or silly to Seon before or even now. The exchange might have turned into a friendly lunch invitation if Seon was interested, but there was something about Aron that made Seon wary. He was too popular, too good-looking, and too well-spoken.

Aron had shown up one day a few weeks ago. Seon knew next to nothing about him, but he spoke with an accent that Seon could never place. That wasn't unusual. This was an international school, and most of the students or their parents were from other countries. His own parents were diplomats. Aron's spiky hair was dyed a vivid and vibrant light electric green. He was tall and lithe but muscular, and it was evident that he could handle himself well. Seon had seen him take on three older boys in a fight apparently to amuse himself.

He could keep the sandwich, Seon decided. He wasn't afraid of Aron but also wasn't interested in playing games with him. He shrugged and walked away.

After school that day, Seon was standing at the corner trying to decide where he wanted to go when he saw Aron coming toward him again. He wondered what interest Aron could have in him since he certainly wasn't one of the popular kids. He nodded to Aron, hoping that the boy would just pass by. They were the same age, so maybe Aron was just being polite.

"Hey," Aron greeted. "Want to grab a coffee? It looks like we're headed the same way."

"I don't know about you," Seon said, "but I wasn't going for coffee."

"Neither was I," Aron said. "But I owe you for the sandwich. Sorry about that. It was a joke, okay. How about a peace offering? Let me make it up to you? Show you I'm not that bad" Otherwise I'll get a reputation."

curious about Aron. There was something different about him. It wasn't just that he was unusual. He didn't fit in, but he wore it like a badge of honor.

In the short time Aron had been at their school, his pranks were already legendary. The teachers didn't yet know who was behind them, but most of the kids in Seon's class seemed to think it was Aron. He'd put blue dye in the gym showers, let all of the rats loose in the science labs, and put all the desks upside down in the teachers' offices. Seon found those pranks boring and juvenile, although the one with the mice had bothered him because he was worried that some of them might get hurt. He'd enjoyed it when Aron filled Miss Caruthers's classroom with flowers. There were hundreds of them, still in pots. There were so many that anyone who wanted a plant had gotten to take one home—student, teacher, or parent. Seon had brought home five.

So, he agreed to walk with Aron. The kid was strange, but maybe not all bad. It was the best way to find out what he really wanted.

Seon gave Aron a sideways glance as they headed toward the coffee shop. He knew the one Aron meant. A lot of kids met there after school since it was only a block away. Seon sometimes stopped in on his way home but never stayed. It felt awkward when he wasn't part of any of the cliques.

"Something on your mind?" Aron said casually.

"Yeah. You," Seon said.

He kept his tone just as casual and his head facing forward. He didn't feel bitter toward Aron for ignoring him before and paying a sudden interest now, but he was curious. The sudden change unnerved him.

Aron turned to look at Seon, raising an eyebrow. The gesture wasn't hostile. Aron seemed more amused.

"Oh, yeah?" Aron asked.

"Yeah," Seon said bluntly. "I was just wondering why you were talking to me all of a sudden. You never have before."

Aron nodded as if acknowledging the logic. "You just seem to be on your own a lot. I thought you could use a friend."

"You've been watching me," Seon asked. That sounded creepy.

"Not *watching you*, watching you. But I've, you know, noticed you. Around. You don't hang out with anyone," Aron said.

Seon nodded. It seemed like a logical enough explanation for what it was worth. Seon preferred to think of himself as neither a loner nor a misfit. He just didn't need people. They were too loud, and their emotions were too much for him. He seemed to know what a person was thinking and feeling just from being around them. Usually. That wasn't working with Aron, and it both bothered him a little and came as a relief. Whereas most people would broadcast their intentions with too much intensity, Aron was a brick wall or at least dampened. Something was leaking through, but if anything, Seon would describe it as curiosity.

"Who needs it?" Seon muttered, finally remembering he hadn't answered Aron.

They had reached the coffee shop. It was packed with teenagers, mostly from their school, as usual. They had shed the trappings of their uniforms and tried to make them look like street clothes. Ties were stuffed into knapsacks, and blazers were either unbuttoned or removed entirely. Aron stayed as he was, but Seon unbuttoned his blazer and loosened his tie. The coffee shop was loud and stuffy.

"So, what'll it be?" Aron asked, winding his way through the crowd to the front cashier. "My treat."

"A chocolate cupcake and a mocha," Seon answered.

As long as he was here, he might as well enjoy it. Seon loved anything sweet, especially chocolate. Aron grinned at his selections and ordered two of each. He handed the cashier a credit card and took the cupcakes. Then they went to stand against the wall to wait for the drinks to be ready.

Seon took a big bite out of his cupcake and then wiped his face with a napkin. It was as delicious as it was disgustingly messy. Aron left to collect the drinks and then, to Seon's relief, led them to a table out on the back patio. It was both quieter and cooler out there.

His preference must have shown on his face because Aron smirked. "I thought you'd like it better out here. You don't seem to like crowds."

Seon shrugged. "It's hot in there." After a moment, he added. "And no, I guess I don't."

"Hey, it's fine," Aron said. "It's always hard to find a table in there this time of day, anyway."

Seon looked around them at that comment. While the inside of the coffee shop was crowded with teenagers and some older young adults, the patio had only a sprinkling of businessmen and a couple of old ladies in a far corner by the fountain, knitting.

"Right," Seon said. He took a sip of his drink.

They sat in silence for a few minutes. Seon could hear the trickling of the fountain and the distant din of the voices from inside. There was even the dull roar of traffic from the street beyond. Nothing from their table.

"Alright, what do you want?" Seon said.

"I have to want something?" Aron said.

"I think you do," Seon said.

"Cards on the table," Aron nodded.

He reached around under the table and pulled out Seon's worn-out leather knapsack. The action was so quick that Seon barely had time to register the movement, let alone try to stop him. Aron had his bag on the table and open by the time Seon even realized what he was doing.

"Hey!" Seon said.

Aron held up a hand to stymie his protests as he reached into the bag and brought out Seon's latest notebook. This one, like all of Seon's other ones, was a scientific journal intended to record observations of his plants. Ever since he'd been young, he'd filled them with records and drawings of plants.

Aron opened the notebook and flipped through the pages. Page after page was filled with drawings of the same image. Images of her. They were all of her. She was in the field. She was carrying buckets of milk. She was looking into the sunrise. None of the sketches showed her face. He still wasn't sure of the details. But they were all her.

"You're a good artist," Aron commented.

Glaring at him, Seon grabbed the notebook. He wasn't sure if Aron would let it go, but he was able to take it back without a fight. As soon as he got his notebook back, Aron grasped it in his hands tightly as if he didn't want to let it go again.

"Who is she?" Aron asked pointedly.

Seon said nothing at first. His head was spinning with the implications that Aron had known what was in his notebook. He didn't think anyone paid that much attention to him. He also didn't know how to describe how he had come to draw those images.

"Nothing," Seon said. "It's nothing."

"You're awfully upset for nothing," Aron pointed out.

"Wouldn't you be if someone went through your belongings and stole from you?" Seon said.

"I didn't steal it," Aron said. "I just borrowed it for a while. You were right here. But yeah, I get it. Sorry, man. I should have asked."

Somewhat mollified, Seon pushed the notebook back into the middle of the table. It seemed silly to hoard it. Aron hadn't really done anything threatening to it. The boy was really more *weird* than anything else. The fact that Seon couldn't sense what he was up to made him confused and flustered.

Looking down at the notebook, Seon wondered whether he should answer Aron's question or not. He still didn't trust Aron. On the other hand, he remembered what he had been thinking before, about how he wished he had someone to tell about the strange presence and how he had visited with her in his dreams.

"I don't have to tell you," Seon finally said.

"No," Aron said. "You don't. I figured you'd want to. That you would want someone to tell."

"Why?" Seon asked. "What makes you think there's anything to tell? How do you know that I didn't just make all this up?" He gestured to the notebook."

Aron gave him a lopsided grin. "Right," he said. "I *might* believe that ... if you weren't acting so serious about this."

Seon had to admit he had a point. On the other hand, anyone would react that way to having a bag snatched and a private, very personal possession like a notebook taken out of it. Seon fell back to glaring at Aron as the boy sat back in his chair with a satisfied grin. That annoyed Seon even more—the fact that he couldn't get a good read on Aron, and Aron seemed to feel like he had Seon all figured out.

"Fine," Seon said. "What do *you* think it is?"

"We-el," Aron said. "I would say these are more than just drawings from your imagination. They mean something."

"What makes you think that?" Seon asked.

"Let's just say I have an idea about it," Aron said.

"Why?" Seon asked. "What do you know about it?"

Aron didn't say anything. Seon stared at his impassive expression, trying to determine what he meant. When Aron didn't give anything away, Seon fought the desire to get up and leave. Part of him wanted to, but part of him wanted to find out what Aron knew or thought he knew.

"If you know something, tell me what you think you know or ask a real question," Seon said. "Otherwise, thanks for the coffee, but I'm leaving."

Seon stood up. He was tempted to put some cash on the table, but that seemed rude. Aron was strange, but Seon didn't really think he deserved rudeness. He'd just invited Seon for coffee and grabbed his notebook. The question itself hadn't been that bad. Seon started to put the notebook back in his bag, but Aron's hand shot up to stop him.

"Maybe we should go somewhere more private, where we can talk about this?" Aron said.

Seon's first instinct was to deny the request, but he found himself nodding. If Aron knew something about this, he wanted to find out what it was. There was something going on, and he wanted to know how Aron was involved. Aron's recent arrival and the mysterious dreams or visits might be connected. If they were, that was what Aron was going to tell him.

"Alright," Seon said carefully. "What did you have in mind?"

Aron nodded and walked out the back gate of the coffee shop. The shop's patio area was in an alley between two high-rise buildings, giving it the illusion of a country setting, complete with a tattered picket fence that Seon supposed had once been white. In reality, the back gate led into an alley littered with garbage where only the toughest weeds grew—weeds that needed barely any sunlight.

Deciding to follow Aron's lead, Seon said nothing as they weaved through the busy streets of the city center, away from the school and downtown metropolis. Soon, they were approaching a park. Seon could remember visiting it a few times on field trips as a child. It was one of the few open green spaces in the city, stretching for four square miles. He immediately felt better. He'd almost forgotten it existed, and he felt like kicking himself for not coming back sooner. Walking into the park was like coming home.

The air seemed cleaner the instant they were faced with the vast stretches of green grass, tall trees, and lazily waving plants. He could see a large pond in the middle of the park with ducks and geese swimming calmly through the clear waters. This place was nearly a paradise. There were a few people here and there, seated on park benches or strolling along talking to each other. The very pace of life seemed slower here—calmer, quieter, with cleaner air. Seon breathed in deeply, closing his eyes and taking it all in.

"Is it in a dome?" Seon said, feeling instantly foolish as he asked. After all, Aron was the visitor here. He rushed over to an informational board near the park's entrance that described its founding and explained how the thousands of trees, plants, and grasses enhanced the air quality in the park and made it cleaner.

"That's amazing," Aron said, reading the sign over Seon's shoulder.

"It is," Seon said. "If we could just get more trees planted around the city, or more plants, we could have better air."

"People don't really seem to care about that," Aron said.

"They should," Seon said, glaring out past the park at the tall high rises and skyscrapers. "The air in this city does more than make people sick. It sucks the life out of a person."

Aron gave Seon a funny look and then nodded. "It's hard to believe you let it get this bad."

"It's not like this where you're from?" Seon said. It was only half the question.

"No," Aron said, in a manner that came out half a snort. "No, where I'm from ...." He let his voice trail off, as if he was trying to decide what to say or maybe how much to say. "No. It's not like this. We do things differently."

"That's good," Seon said. "I think I'd like to go somewhere like that. I'd like to see that. I don't like ... I hate the air here. I am sometimes more at home with plants or animals than people."

Seon was surprised at himself for being so blunt, but Aron smiled. Seon thought it might have been the first genuine smile he'd seen from him. He didn't respond to the comment. He just walked off into the park, toward the pond. Seon followed.

"Why are you here?" Seon asked when they reached a bench near the pond. No one else was on this side of the pond, so they had the area primarily to themselves. "Is your family in the Diplomatic Corps?"

"You could say that," Aron said. "I travel around a lot."

The answer seemed evasive, but Seon nodded. He didn't want Aron prying into his personal life, so it seemed just as well that he didn't either pry into Aron's. There was a faraway look in Aron's eye that was a bit unusual, so Seon decided to keep quiet and wait for him to say what he was about.

"I did ask you here for a reason," Aron said. "I know the girl in your notebook. Or at least, I know of her."

"You know *of* her," Seon asked.

Of all of the things Aron might say, that was the last thing he expected. He'd thought maybe Aron was just interested in art or maybe liked him or something. Seon didn't bend that way and was only curious about who Aron was. This was crazy. It made him think he'd heard wrong.

"What do you mean you know of her?" Seon repeated, as a question this time, to make sure he'd heard right.

"That's a long story," Aron said. "I really can't get into all the details. As in, I *really* can't get into them. Just trust me on that. I can tell you that she's real, and she's trying to contact you, and I need your help."

Chapter 3

Seon stared at Aron. He knew that he probably looked like an idiot, staring blankly, but his life had turned into a science fiction movie or a fantasy book in one afternoon. He would need some time to process that. After all, it's not just any day that a kid you barely know comes up to you and says he knows the girl you'd been visiting almost nightly in your dreams and says he needs to find her.

"Umm," Seon said, producing this very intelligent answer after staring for so long he felt he had to say something. "Are you sure?"

"Yes, I'm sure," Aron said, with no trace of teasing in his tone. "Why do you think I'm here?"

That might have meant here in this park, here in this city, or here on this planet. Seon had a feeling it might have meant all three. He thought he might have started to look a little bug-eyed by now, so he closed his eyes and looked down, deciding to count to ten and then open his eyes. If Aron was still there, at least some of this was real.

He was still there. Sitting on the park bench. Looking at Seon with an amused cockeyed grin as if he knew exactly what he had just done. Oh well, Seon had probably done stranger things. That was why most people gave him a wide berth. He was the kid who talked to plants and could make animals do things he wanted. The chances of Aron thinking of him as not a freak would be practically zero, except that it seemed that it was why Aron had sought him out in the first place.

And it hadn't scared him off yet.

"Why *are* you here?" Seon asked.

"I need to find her," Aron said. "And I need your help to do it."

Well. That was an interesting development.

"What makes you think I can find her?" Seon asked. "What makes you think I even know who she is? And if I did, what makes you think I would help you? I don't know you. You could be dangerous. You could be dangerous to her."

"How do you know she isn't dangerous?" Aron asked.

He had a point there. Seon didn't know anything of the kind. He hadn't even seen a clear image of her face, and the eyes were supposedly the window into the soul. He could feel her emotions though, just as with everyone else. Well, not quite as with everyone else. Hers were both stronger and not as strong. It was as if, with her, he felt what she *wanted* him to feel.

Hmm. Aron might have a point. That did seem a little manipulative. Then again, Seon couldn't feel much from Aron, so he didn't trust him either.

"I know you don't trust me," Aron said, apparently reading what Seon had been thinking. "I have something to show you. It might help you understand."

He reached into his pack, a worn leather sack that was both similar to ones Seon had seen others use and utterly unique at the same time, and brought out what looked like a clay or ceramic tile. It reminded Seon of images he had seen from history lessons. Aron slid it over to Seon, and he picked it up.

The tile was slightly worn and shiny. It was cool to the touch and weighed very little. It was thin—almost as thin as a piece of paper, yet so strong that Seon was sure it wouldn't break if he dropped it. The texture was more like clay, but the surface on the front reminded him of ceramic due to its sheen. It had been glazed. It was the image of a girl. The girl.

It was the first time he'd ever seen her face clearly, but he would recognize her anywhere. In his sketches, he had tried a few times to get her eyes right or the shape of her nose. He had even tried to sketch in a general mouth. It was never right. This was it, though. It was perfect. It was her.

"Where did you get this?" Seon said in a low breath.

"Is that her?" Aron asked. "Is that the girl from your sketches?"

"Before I tell you that," Seon said, "Aron, you have to tell me where you got this!"

Aron nodded as if he had expected this demand. He said nothing for a moment. Then he gestured at Seon's bag, a request for permission this time. Seon nodded, barely taking his eyes off the tile. Aron took the notebook and opened it to one of the sketches, laying it down on the bench next to the tile. Side by side, the resemblance was striking, even with Seon's incomplete sketches.

"You really are a talented artist," Aron commented.

"Enough of that!" Seon said. "Where did you get it?"

"Where did you get these images?" Aron pointed to the notebook.

They were at an impasse, and Seon knew it. He did not want to explain about her, yet, even with a picture in his hand. Aron clearly knew more about this than he was telling. There was more to Aron than he was telling. Seon was already mixed up in this, whether he liked it or not. He had been since the first time he had met with this girl. He could walk away now. He *should* walk away now.

But something was stopping him.

She was doing this to him. She was compelling him, somehow, to come night after night to that field and talk to her. She spoke to him in his mind, with emotions instead of words, and he came. He was becoming obsessed. He didn't think he was in love with her, exactly, but she was becoming all that he thought about. Fourteen was not too young to fall for someone, especially someone who, Seon had to admit, was quite a knockout. There was more to this than that. She *needed* him; he knew that. He just didn't know what she needed. That was what worried him. He wasn't comfortable being a part of this with incomplete information.

He was used to knowing more about people than they were prepared to divulge. He was *not* used to being on the lesser end of the bargain. This process was really getting to him.

And yet, something made him stop and think that this was his one chance to end it. The late-night visits, whether in his dreams or in his head, would go on if he didn't do something. Aron had the answers.

"I see her sometimes," Seon began slowly, not sure how to say it. "I guess I meet with her. In my dreams. It's not like a dream. It's more of a ... projection. I don't know how to explain it. I just know that it's real. She calls to me. It's like I don't have a choice to go. Or maybe at one time I didn't, but now I ... I just go. Not every night, but a lot. And I don't see her face, or I don't remember it. This is the first time ...."

He realized he was rambling. His words sounded hollow and incoherent even to his own ears. He didn't look at Aron. Instead, he looked down at the tile and at his notebook. It was still hard to believe that this was happening. That it was real. That she was real. He had known it all along, had wanted to believe it, but the confirmation was something else entirely.

"Yeah, I get it," Aron said. "It makes sense."

"It does?" Seon had no idea how it could.

"Sure," Aron said. "I'll have to explain that to you another time. Look, there's a lot I'd like to explain, but I really can't, yet. Not here or now. I will soon if you want me to. I just needed to know if you were legit. It looks like you are. You're the one we've been looking for."

Seon stared at him. "Looking for? Who's we? What are you talking about?"

"Yeah, I have to explain that later too. You should come with me. I can introduce you to someone who can tell you a lot more," Aron said.

He was a lot calmer than Seon felt he had a right to be. Seon did not feel calm at all. His head was spinning. Aron was talking nonsense. The whole thing was starting to seem like a setup.

"What are you talking about," Seon said. "I'm not going anywhere with you. Introduce me? Who? What are you talking about?"

"It's cool," Aron said. "I get that it all sounds strange. That's why you should come with me. I can't do what you can, man. I can't get you to come with me. You'll just have to come if you want to."

"What?" Seon stared. "What do you mean, 'what I can'? What can I do?"

"Never mind," Aron said easily. "Look, it's simple. You have something you want to know. There's only one way you'll get it. If you want to find out, it's up to you."

With that, he stood up and started walking away. Seon stayed where he was, on the park bench looking out at the ducks, for almost a full minute before he got up and marched after Aron. He grabbed the other boy by the arm, realizing as he did so that Aron was every bit as muscular as he looked. This kid was strong, and if he wanted to go, there was nothing Seon could do to stop him. He could deck Seon and have him laid out on the ground in seconds. Seon continued. He needed answers.

"No," Seon insisted. "You're not getting off that easy. You started this. You have to tell me what is going on."

"You're right," Aron said, stopping but not turning around. He tilted his head slightly back at Aron. "I told you what you need to do to get answers. That is what I have to offer you. You're not going to get them from me here and now."

"Why?" Seon demanded. "Why not?"

"Well, for one thing," Aron said. "It's not safe. We have no idea who's listening."

Seon looked around. As far as he could see, it was just the two of them. A long way off, three teens were walking in the park. Even further out was a pair of elderly men walking a dog. None of the people scattered throughout the park could hear them as far as he could tell. He looked back at Aron skeptically.

"Believe me, there are ways to listen in without being close," Aron said.

Seon nodded. He had seen parabolic microphones used on television. Then he had to resist the urge to scoff or laugh out loud. There was nothing they could possibly say that would be that important. Instead, he stared down at his feet. He was starting to feel in over his head. Either this was Aron's cruelest prank yet, or his life had just gotten much more interesting.

"Fine," Seon said, almost spitting the word. "Say I believe you. What do I do?"

"Meet me at the corner of One Hundred Twenty-Fifth and Bertram Street at Seven Thirty," Aron said. "I will wait no longer than half an hour. If you're there, I will know you're interested. If you're not, then, well, we'll see."

"What do you mean, 'we'll see,' Aron?" Seon said.

Instead of responding, Aron just gave Seon the crooked grin he had come to expect and found increasingly annoying. Seon glared back, something he also found himself doing more and more in Aron's presence. He barely knew this kid, and their relationship seemed to have gotten off on an adversarial note.

"I am not guaranteeing anything," Seon said," except that I don't like the sound of this."

"I can't promise anything else," Aron said. "If you want to know more, you'll just have to meet me then."

Seon let go of Aron's arm. He'd just realized he was still holding it. With a growing feeling of frustration, he watched Aron lope off like he didn't have a care in the world. He doubted that was the case. He was pretty sure Aron's outer façade was ninety percent act. Whatever was going on inside, Aron was anything but an open book.

In the meantime, Seon had a decision to make. If he was living a spy novel, he would have said it was a trap. His life was nothing like that. He led a dull existence where he went to a stuffy school where most of the kids were alright, but some were rich snobs, and some were seriously messed up because their parents were politicians or diplomats. Aron might fall into that category. This might be how he got his kicks, making up complicated games.

It didn't explain how he knew about the girl. He might have gotten ahold of one of Seon's sketchbooks somehow, and this was an elaborate prank. Somehow, it didn't seem like that. Aron always had an air of someone who knew something. He also had walls that Seon both admired because his emotions didn't leak out like the rest of humanity and feared because he knew he couldn't tell what Aron was thinking. That worried him.

Seon decided the best thing to do was to stay in the park. For the next while, he wandered around thinking. He enjoyed the different plants. Most of them were so healthy. It was such an inspiration to be in a place like this. He felt free for the first time.

Suddenly, he heard laughter coming from behind some bushes off the path up ahead. It wasn't pleasant laughter. It was the kind of laughter that came from kids who were hurting someone and enjoying it. He could feel that enjoyment in the violence rolling off them in waves.

Picking up his pace, Seon hurried over until he was nearly running. When he got there, the sight almost sickened him. A group of teens around his own age surrounded what looked like a bird, poking at it with sticks. The poor thing was flapping one wing and hopping around.

"Hey!" Seon called out to them. "What are you doing? Stop that!"

For some reason, seeing him stopped them. They grinned at him and ran off, dropping their sticks as they went. Seon had no idea why they left. He had been prepared to fight them off. Maybe Aron was on to something, and he could make people do what he wanted.

With as much care as he could, Seon approached the bird. He knelt beside it carefully so as not to spook the creature. It was a beautiful red-tailed hawk, a juvenile. By the looks of it, one wing was broken, and the other was badly sprained. Seon was filled with loathing for the group of boys and half-wanted to run after them and get revenge. He despised people who tortured animals for sport.

"It's okay, girl," Seon said soothingly.

There was little he could do here. It occurred to him that the best thing would be to take it to a veterinarian, preferably a zoo. He knew of a zoo in the city, but it would take hours to get there, even by public transportation or taxi. His best chance would be to try to quiet the little bird first. If he could find a local vet, they might be able to make the hawk comfortable enough for transport.

Seon stroked her feathers and clucked at her soothingly, and then carefully picked her up. He was surprised she let him. Somehow, he knew she would. He had always had a way with animals, far beyond the ability to train them. He hadn't spent as much time with wild animals, but apparently, the affinity translated to them as well.

Carefully, Seon carried the bird the few feet to the closest park bench and sat down. He placed her onto his lap and then held his hands over her wings. He wasn't sure why he felt like this would calm her down, but instinctively he seemed to think it would be the best idea. When it came to plants and animals and what to do for them, Seon had learned long ago to trust his instincts. Doing so usually worked, and not doing so proved disastrous.

Sometime later, Seon woke with a start. He was still on the park bench. He had the young hawk on his lap. She was asleep peacefully, with his hands placed over her injured wings. He wasn't sure how long he stayed that way. In fact, he must have been in the park for hours. It was now dark, and all the street lamps in the park were on creating large swaths of light and lurking shadows.

Seon wasn't able to move his hands to reach into his pocket and find his phone to see what time it was, and he didn't wear a watch. He knew he had missed the time he was supposed to have met with Aron. He couldn't decide if that was a good thing or a bad thing. At the moment, he was more than a little disturbed at having fallen asleep in the park. That didn't seem like the safest thing to do.

"Ah, here he is," Aron said.

To Seon, it sounded like a voice coming out of the darkness. He tried to turn his head to see where Aron was, but he couldn't see him at first. Then Aron came into view. Next to him was a man. The man was old enough to be Aron's father but looked nothing like him except that he also seemed fit and muscular. He was tall, lean, and had a chiseled face with a trimmed gray beard. His hair was also gray, cut in a short, severe, military-style cut and his expression was stern. He seemed the opposite of Aron in every way. This man was tight in all the ways Aron was loose.

"Hey," Aron said. "You didn't come, and I started to worry. I thought you might still be here, so I came looking for you."

With a glance at the man standing next to Aron, whose penetrating glance was taking in Seon and the hawk silently, Seon just stared back at Aron. He wasn't sure what to say. Aron had left him on a bit of a sour note, and then he showed up here with this man with no introduction. Seon was feeling more perturbed and confused than ever.

"I never said I'd come," Seon said.

"All the same," Aron said, ignoring the acidity in Seon's tone. "It looks like you did get into something."

"Not really," Seon said. He was beginning to feel that this conversation was absurd.

Finally, the man spoke.

"Where did you get the hawk?" he asked.

"Some boys were torturing her," Aron said, not sure why he even answered. "She has a broken wing, and I think the other one's sprained."

"And she let you pick her up and hold her like that?" the man asked. "For how long?"

"Umm," Seon said. "Well, it was right after Aron left, actually. I don't know, I guess I fell asleep. I didn't mean to. I was just going to sit down with her for a minute to calm her down and then … well, I don't know what happened, exactly. I just woke up a minute ago."

"Let's see her," the man said.

"What do you mean?" Seon asked. "I don't mean to be rude, but who are you? Who is he?"

The last question was directed at Aron in a quiet voice. Seon had barely noticed that Aron had lurked closer and closer during the interrogation until he was kneeling next to Seon, inspecting the bird. He had moved so stealthily that she hadn't even woken up.

"He's alright," Aron answered, whispering as well so as not to disturb the bird. "His name's Corin."

"That doesn't answer my question," Seon answered in a fierce whisper.

All the talking seemed to have finally awakened the little hawk. She wobbled and stretched her wings out with a squawk. Seon gasped, afraid she would hurt herself. Somehow, though, both wings were fine.

"They're not broken," he said.

"Are you sure they were broken?" Aron asked.

"One of them was for sure," Seon said, carefully manipulating the right wing, making sure there were no signs of a break. "I think the other one was injured, maybe sprained."

"You healed her," Corin said.

"What?" Seon asked, bewildered.

"You have done something like this before," he told Seon as if this was a fact Seon should have known.

Seon just stared at the man and then looked at Aron. These

two strangers would have to stop telling him things about himself that they knew that he was supposed to know but didn't. It was getting on his nerves.

"No," Seon insisted. "I haven't."

"You have," Corin. "I'm sure if you think about it, you will remember. You have not come to this level of skill without doing it before. Still, it took something out of you. That's why you fell asleep. Also, some of it is still subconscious. It worked better when you were asleep."

"Right," Seon muttered absentmindedly. That made no sense to him.

"Do you think she can fly?" Aron asked.

"I don't know," Seon said. "I have no idea what is going on here. I just sat down on a park bench with an injured hawk and woke up with one that was, well, not."

"Well," Aron said with a lopsided grin, "let's try it."

Seon nodded. Part of him was afraid to see if the little hawk could fly, and part of him just didn't want to let her go. It was silly because he knew she was a wild thing and belonged out there flying. He stood up and tossed her into the air. To his surprise and delight, she did start to fly.

The three of them watched as the little hawk began with lazy circles above their heads and then moved on to larger and larger loops, flying around the treetops. Seon grinned, and Aron clapped him on the back in congratulation. Seon felt the beginning of tears come to his eyes and blinked them back. He was happy she was healed. He'd thought the little hawk was a goner for sure.

When he watched her fly like that, zigging and zagging through the air, there was no way he could resent her leaving. She was truly happy, and that was all that mattered. He was just relieved to see that she was better and that her run-in with those horrors hadn't ended in tragedy.

Then the strangest thing happened. Her loops began to get smaller and smaller and lower and lower. She came closer to him, and he whistled at her, trying to tell her that he was pleased that she was healthy and that she should enjoy her freedom. The opposite happened. She came careening in and landed on the strap of his leather knapsack.

Seon felt his heart swell with relief and pride. He reached into the outer pocket of his knapsack where he had a bag of dried fruit, removed a piece, and held it out for her. He felt terrible about not having remembered it before. She had probably been hungry. She devoured the fruit as he stroked her feathers.

"Well," Aron said, "I guess you have a familiar."

Seon snorted and grinned at the hawk. That was an old-fashioned term, used in fairy tales and fantasy novels with witches and wizards. It was just another way Aron was a little bit off. He didn't say anything about that.

"She does seem to like me," Seon said.

"What are you going to name her?" Aron said.

"Oh, I have no idea," Seon said, not taking the question seriously since the hawk wasn't his to name. "What do you suggest?"

"Alix," Aron said confidently. "It means protector."

"Okay," Seon said. "If you stick around," he told the hawk, "I will call you Alix."

Seon could have sworn that the bird understood him and agreed with his choice of name. She stayed on the strap of his knapsack and preened her feathers. Seon just laughed and shook his head. He was glad he had a knapsack with such a thick strap; otherwise, her talons would be digging into his shoulder.

"You'll want to get a glove for sure," Corin said, "or a shoulder pad."

Seon nodded, gently stroking Alix's feathers. When he looked into her eyes, he could have sworn that she was intelligent. She seemed to trust him and be perfectly content to stay with him. It was amazing.

At the moment, he had another problem, though. Aron had brought Corin to him, thus taking away any choice he might have otherwise had. He wasn't sure how much he trusted Aron, but he knew immediately that he trusted Corin less. He could sense nothing from the man, and his facial expression was just as blank. He exuded sternness and competence because that was the image he wanted the world to see. Seon had no idea who he really was.

"Well," Seon said, finally facing them, "what do you want from me?"

Chapter 4

"As you were told earlier, we will not discuss it out in the open here," Corin told him.

There was no rebuke in the tone, but it was blunt. Seon was coming to realize that Corin was a fairly blunt person. He usually liked that, at least when people were honest about who they were and what they really wanted.

So Seon nodded. "I'm not going to go with you somewhere I don't know," he said. "I don't know you at all, and I barely know Aron."

That seemed reasonable to Seon. After all, if this was a spy novel, his character would have taken these precautions. Bilbo Baggins wouldn't want to go off until he'd had supper and made sure the adventure wasn't too dangerous. Seon wanted to know who these people were, where they had come from, and why they seemed to know more about him than he knew about himself. He was going nowhere with them until they told him that.

"He has a point, Sir," Aron said. "Maybe there are a few things that are safe to say. Things everyone already knows. Except for Seon, of course."

Seon glared at him, wondering what he meant by that. Aron made it sound like someone was indeed watching them, listening to the conversation. It was absurd. Both of these two were paranoid. Seon would have decidedly called it a prank if there wasn't an adult involved. Corin didn't look like the type to get in on any of Aron's shenanigans. In fact, if this was Aron's father, he'd hate to see what happened to Aron if he ever found out about any of the hijinks his son got into at school. Maybe it gave Seon leverage.

Despite the potential for blackmailing Aron into telling him something, Seon highly doubted it would work out in his favor. Something strange was going on here, and it was much bigger than a father getting upset at his son for messing with the football team's jerseys. It was time to find out.

While these thoughts were going through his head, Seon noticed that Aron and Corin were exchanging some kind of nonverbal conversation. That is, they were staring at each other, and occasionally Corin would raise an eyebrow just a smidge, or Aron would smirk. Seon had no idea how, but they were talking to each other, and it wasn't through body language. They were both completely closed off from him. Aron was more closed off than usual. Seon couldn't sense a thing from him. Weird.

As suddenly as it began, the little silent talk ended. Seon waited for the outcome. Corin sent one more look toward Aron that didn't seem conciliatory and then turned to Seon.

"We will meet in a neutral, co-selected location that is unlikely to be monitored," he said.

"Okay," Seon said. "Do you have a suggestion?"

"As the disputing party, the first suggestion goes to you," Corin said.

The disputing party, Seon figured, must mean that he refused to go anywhere alone with the two of them. In that case, he tried to wrap his brain around where they could go that no one else might be.

"Okay," Seon said. "How about my parents' apartment? I mean my apartment. I know where the panic button is if you try anything, and there's security. I'm sure you're not afraid of me. And I doubt anyone's watching or listening to me."

"No," Corin said.

"No?" Seon said. "Why not?"

"Your identity is not well-known, but it is not inconceivable that we are the first to locate you," Corin said, in the manner of explaining something to a small child. "We cannot take the risk that you are under surveillance. Also, given your parents' professions, I am sure they take measures to prevent it. Still, other parties may have attempted surveillance, and we cannot risk them selling the information."

"Wow," Seon said, looking at Aron. "Okay. What is your suggestion then?"

Corin looked to Aron expectantly. Seon was curious to see what he would come up with. Aron definitely seemed like a divergent thinker.

"The school," Aron said.

"The school?" Seon said.

"Yes," Aron said. "It's open at night, but it's mostly just the custodians and some teachers there. It will be easy to find an empty classroom to talk in. The school has excellent security, but since we are students, there won't be any problem for us getting in. It's perfect."

Seon turned to Corin to see if he would turn down this idea. Instead, Corin nodded. Seon was surprised, but he could see Aron's logic. It did seem like a good plan.

"Very well," Corin said. "We will go to the school. You will tell them that it is a parent-teacher meeting we are attending. Aron, do you have a room in mind?"

"Yes, Sir," Aron said with a slight nod. "There is a row of disused classrooms on the fourth floor. They are still kept in good repair and often used for meetings, but not every day. We can slip in and out easily."

Seon nodded. He knew the rooms Aron was talking about. Kids used to meet up there for pranks or to make out or engage in other activities where they didn't want to get caught, so the school kept them locked now.

"They're locked," Seon said.

"Not a problem," Aron said confidently.

Seon shrugged. If Aron had stolen a key code, that was his lookout. He followed the two of them out of the park. Corin hailed a cab, and they were soon on their way to the school. No one said a word on the way. The driver didn't mention the fact that Seon had a red-tailed hawk on his shoulder.

When they got to the school, Corin greeted the officer at the security desk. He sounded so authoritative that Seon almost believed what he said about them being there to meet with his sons' teachers. If the man realized that neither of the kids were Corin's sons and didn't look remotely like him or like each other, he chose not to let on.

By now, Seon was convinced that there was no familial relationship between these two. That made him trust them less. For one thing, it seemed like Aron would have introduced the man as his father instead of by name. He wasn't even bothering to pretend they had that kind of relationship. They acted like secret agents on a mission. There was something strange about the two of them and whatever they were into, Seon was already in pretty deep.

In no time, they were upstairs, and Aron walked right up to one of the classrooms and opened the door. Seon saw that he just held his hand on the door lock and it unlocked. So, he hadn't stolen a key; he just had a way to unlock it without needing one. It was a handy trick.

The three of them settled down at a table in the middle of the room. No one said anything for a few minutes. They just looked at each other. It was unnerving. Finally, Seon couldn't stand it anymore. He figured he was showing some kind of weakness by speaking first, but he didn't care.

"So, did you check the room for bugs?

The quip did nothing to lighten the mood. Aron and Corin just stared back at him. Corin's face was blank and unreadable as always, and Aron's had a hint of a wry smile of appreciation but nothing more. Seon tried again.

"Look, I don't know what you want from me. I don't know who she is or how to reach her," Seon began.

"We know who she is," Corin said. "What we don't know is where she is. That is where you come in."

"How? I don't contact her. She contacts me," Seon said.

"That may change," Corin said. "With time and training, you may be able to contact her and communicate with her. You are already getting stronger."

"How do you know this? What makes you think I can do any of the things you say I can do?" Seon asked.

For Seon, that was the cusp of the argument. He knew that something was changing inside of him. He could feel a connection to Alix and maybe even to these two strangers. That did not mean he trusted them. The more they told him he could do, the more he doubted he could do it.

"We know," Corin said simply.

"How do you know?" Seon asked. "Where did you two come from, anyway? Are you from another planet or something?"

"No," Corin said. "We are from another land."

"Another land?" Seon said, getting a queasy feeling in his stomach at the thought of it. "What does that even mean? How do you expect me to believe any of this without proof?"

"Proof?" Aron said in an irritated tone. "Why do you need

proof? Did you not see what you did today? Is that not proof enough?"

Seon looked at Corin, expecting him to rebuke his younger compatriot for interrupting him. He remained impassive, apparently waiting for Seon to respond to Aron's question. Seon looked down, staring at his hands. It had been an extraordinary feat, but he hadn't even been conscious when he did it. He didn't really know it wasn't a trick.

"I can't explain that," Seon said. "Anyway, I don't remember it. It might not have happened that way."

"What way?" Aron said. "How do you think it happened?"

"You have extraordinary abilities," Corin said, interrupting Aron without looking at him.

"We call them Gifts. Your people might call them 'powers' or magic. It all amounts to the same thing. You can do things people can't. You can see into others' minds. Feel their emotions. Push their thoughts. Make them do what you want to."

"Now wait a minute," Seon began, about to tell Corin that he could do nothing of the sort.

Corin held him off with a raised palm. Seon stopped to let him finish. He might as well let them tell him what they came for.

"You can influence plants and animals," Corin continued. "You can make plants grow faster, or the way you want them to. You can make animals do your bidding. You can also heal any living thing."

The gravity with which Corin spoke, especially the last part, held in the room for several moments. When he said it like that, Seon felt unworthy of these Gifts. They seemed much too precious to waste on someone as uninteresting as him. He looked down, suddenly embarrassed.

"You have a rare Gift, Seon," Corin said, "not to be taken lightly. That is one of the reasons why we came here to find you. Because you can also communicate with people and animals, even across great distances. You have been doing it for months."

"*I* have been doing it?" Seon said, trying to hold off his disbelief.

"You have both been communicating," Corin clarified. "She needed to find one who had your Gift, and it is rare. She went to a great deal of trouble to find you."

"How did she find me?" Seon asked.

"By reaching out, I imagine," Corin said. "Your powers are strong but have mostly been dormant."

"Powers," Seon shook his head. "I don't understand."

"You're a *tractatori,* Seon," Aron said. "And here! There hasn't been a Gifted for a thousand years in ...."

"Let's focus on the task at hand," Corin said suddenly, cutting Aron off.

Seon wondered what Aron had been about to say and why he'd been interrupted. It seemed to him that the 'task at hand' was telling Seon what was going on and who they were and where they were from, and he wasn't pleased with Corin disrupting that process. Corin was way too cagey for Seon's taste.

"What is a *trac* ...," Seon gave up, trying to repeat the jumble of sounds Aron had said with such reverence. "Whatever. What am I, and what does it mean?"

"I told you what it means," Corin said, apparently beginning to lose patience. "I also told you what is at stake here. We need to find the girl, and we need to do it now."

"Actually, you didn't," Seon said. He knew that Aron spoke respectfully to Corin, and he was being pretty rude, but he was past caring. He wasn't answering to anyone in this shindig. "You just made me meet with you and spouted a bunch of nonsense that you really haven't proved, and no one has really told me anything about the girl I have been dreaming about. Who is she? Is she in trouble? Why? Why is she trying to reach me? Does she have the same gifts as me?"

As far as Seon was concerned, those were all perfectly legitimate questions. He had more questions too, but they were all competing for space in his brain, and those were the ones that popped out first. The rest would have to pop out later.

"She is not 'in trouble,' per se," Corin said, "but she does need our help. She apparently reached out to you, and you can communicate with her, so we need you."

"What do you mean, 'you need me?'" Seon said.

"Aron and I are leaving tomorrow to go ... find her," Corin said. "We need you to come with us because we don't know where she is."

"Oh, no," Seon said, shaking his head. "No way. I am not coming with two people I just met to go rescue some girl I don't know, to someplace I have never heard of that might be on another planet."

What he didn't add was that they scared him. Aron was built like a tank, despite being lean and lanky. Seon knew that under his clean-cut appearance, Corin could probably knock Seon over the head and haul him off without a second thought. He was beginning to regret ever having agreed to this meeting. The school no longer seemed as safe.

"I have to go," Seon said, standing up quickly. Alix let out a squawk at the sudden movement.

"So soon?" Corin asked, his voice so low it almost sounded like a purr. He stood up, along with Aron.

Was that Seon's imagination, or did Corin sound amused? Seon hadn't known Corin long, but he didn't rate an amused Corin high on his list of experiences. Corin seemed like the type to laugh at car wrecks.

"Seon, it'll be fine," Aron said, his voice half-placating and half-resigned.

This was not good. Seon looked around. He realized that there was a camera in the corner of the room, but the blinking light that usually indicated it was on was not blinking. That meant the camera was off. Seon didn't need to wonder why. He looked at Aron.

"Oh, yeah, I turned it off when we first came in," Aron said casually, noticing Seon looking at the camera and then at him.

"You did?" Seon was afraid his voice came out almost a squawk. "How?"

"Like this," Aron waved his hand, and most of the lights in the room went out, except for one next to the side door. Seon felt his heart sink. "Care to reconsider? You really will be better off if you come with us quietly."

Seon glared at Aron. Somehow, the boy didn't seem mean-spirited even when he was making an outright threat. Seon looked over to Corin. He was standing casually halfway between the side door and the table, blocking Seon's exit. Seon knew it was no use. They were both too fast and too strong for him.

"I guess I will go with you," Seon said. "Do I have a choice? This is kidnapping." The last part was directed at Corin.

"He never worries about minor details," Aron said as he grabbed Seon's arm and pushed him toward the door.

Chapter 5

They left the building through back hallways while Aron lazily misdirected or turned off any security cameras they happened to pass. Seon didn't know why they bothered, since he had hastily written a message telling his parents that he was going on a school trip. He'd had no time and put barely any effort into it, since he'd had to write it as they were walking. They were outside in minutes, and Corin was at the end of the narrow alley between the school and the office building next door before the two of them were even through the exit.

"Where is he going?" Seon asked Aron quietly.

On the one hand, Seon thought he could make a break for it. Corin was obviously the bigger threat. If he had no intention of staying with these two because he didn't believe their story or just didn't buy into their plan, now was the time to run. Corin was gone and that left only Aron.

It was obvious that Aron was no pushover though. Seon had no training in evasion or fighting and had never spent any time in a weights room outside of when it was required in school for a minor credit class. He didn't consider himself strong or brave. He wasn't even sure why we wanted to get away so badly. Aron could beat the snot out of him with one hand, of that he was absolutely sure.

Seon noticed Aron seemed to be slowing down near the entrance to a narrow alley between two buildings. At first it seemed like it was because he suspected Seon of something, but it soon became obvious that instead, Aron seemed to be listening or using some kind of sense that Seon didn't possess. Now Seon was suddenly nervous for an entirely different reason. Something was about to go down and he had no idea what.

"What is it?" Seon asked in a near-whisper, not wanting to break Aron's concentration but unable to resist the urge to grab his arm.

Aron shook his head slightly, not even trying to shake Seon off and instead focusing on the edge of the building. He did not turn the corner, and instead stood there listening.

There was nothing for moments, and then Aron jumped back when a burst of what looked like blue lightning came whizzing past him, narrowly missing him even though he hadn't even turned the corner. Seon was sure it was the momentary distraction he had given Aron that had caused his concentration to falter. He was ready to run in the opposite direction, but Aron surprised him by heading toward the shots instead of away.

"What are you doing?" Seon demanded.

Aron held up a hand and bolted around the building, as if his palm alone could stop whoever or whatever was firing at them. Seon thought he had lost his mind, but decided there was no way he was following him even though he was tempted to pull him back. His best bet was to hope the guy knew what he was doing.

A few minutes after Aron went around the corner, Seon carefully peeked after him. There was no sign of who or what had been shooting, but Aron was hunched over on the ground in the alleyway. After waiting as long as he dared, Seon rushed over to him.

"Aron," Seon said tentatively, feeling around for a pulse. "Aron!"

He got no response, but Seon was afraid to move the boy. He could not find any blood and there did not seem to be an obvious injury of any kind, but Aron was unconscious. Seon was not even sure how to reach Corin to get help. Calling the police or an ambulance seemed like a bad idea if these people really were from some other world and Aron had just been injured in a magic fight Seon knew nothing about.

In the best compromise Seon could think of, he started going through Aron's pockets. His clothes were the same as Seon's since they were both wearing the standard school uniform. There was nothing in his pockets, but in his book bag, Seon found a communication device he recognized. He hoped it wasn't password activated.

After fiddling with it for a few minutes, Seon found what looked like a list of contacts. On his device, there weren't a lot, his friends, brothers, and parents were all listed. Aron had one contact. That made it easy. It had to be Corin. Seon dialed. A voice answered that he recognized as Corin's, speaking in a language he definitely did not recognize.

"Corin? It's Seon," Seon spoke as clearly and calmly as he could, trying not to sound nervous. "Something's happened. Aron's hurt. He got ... shot? I have no idea really. We're in an alley near the school. Where are you? I have no idea what to do because Aron's unconscious. I can't leave him here."

"Stay there. Keep cover. I'm coming shortly," Corin ordered.

After Corin hung up, Seon put the device in his pocket and resisted screaming in frustration. He looked down and noticed that Aron was stirring. Seon dropped to his knees, trying to comfort the boy.

"Aron? Can you hear me? Are you okay? What happened?"

As soon as the words left his lips, Seon felt like an idiot for voicing them. Of course Aron was not okay and he wasn't going to tell Seon what happened. Seon wanted to shake Aron, but didn't do that either. He just gently tried to hold his head up.

Aron groaned.

"Corin's coming," Seon reassured him. "I used your ... I called him. I hope that's alright."

It seemed like Aron was struggling even more to sit up. Seon couldn't blame him. Corin had not sounded happy and Seon didn't want to be in the middle of whatever was going on, but he had the feeling he already was. He had been ever since the mystery girl started calling him in his dreams.

"Look, just stay still," Seon pleaded.

Aron glared at him, then held his head in his hands. It wasn't long after that when Corin came purposefully down the alley. Seon had not mistaken the mood he was in. He was incensed. Seon scrambled to his feet and got out of the way as soon as Corin appeared on the scene. The older man barely spared a glance his way and instead glowered at Aron.

"Can you get up?"

"Yes, Sir," Aron said, in a voice that did not sound at all convincing to Seon.

Corin stood there with his arms crossed while Aron struggled to his feet. Although Seon wanted to help, he didn't dare. He watched as Aron stood up and winced, then carefully walked out of the alley with Corin just behind him. As far as Seon could tell, Aron was just barely holding it together. He must have been knocked out by the injury, but Seon still hadn't been able to locate it and Corin was apparently leaving any discussion of or treatment of it for later.

Fortunately, the awkward procession was short because Corin had a cab waiting at the end of the alley. He stood just off to the side, waiting like a sentry, while the two of them got in. It occurred to Seon that Corin might be afraid that whoever had attacked might be coming back to finish them off, so he got into the cab as quickly as he could. As soon as he was in the back seat with Aron, Corin got into the passenger side and they were off.

There was no sound made by anyone as they drove, and Seon kept his eyes on Aron. He was leaning back against the vinyl seats and looked almost as pale as the cream-colored interior. Seon couldn't see Corin from where they were seated, but he was anxious to find out what was wrong with Aron. Clearly Corin was not the coddling type.

"What happened to you?" Seon asked in a low voice.

For a moment, Seon didn't think Aron would answer. Then he heard a low gurgling sound that he realized was a sort of chortle. Apparently Aron was somewhat amused by the situation.

"I was an idiot," Aron answered blunty, loudly enough for Corin to hear. "I should have never tried it."

"What?" Seon was getting as frustrated as he was curious. "What did you try? Stopping lightning with your bare hands?"

This comment earned Seon a strange look from Aron, which almost seemed to be respect. Aron shrugged, and then leaned his head back against the car seat again. He sighed.

"Something like that," he murmured.

"Did you get ... burnt or something?" Seon asked.

In response, Aron lifted up the side of his leather jacket to reveal a large, reddish-purple burn. It was white in the middle and backend on the edges. Seon leaned over and stared at it in horror and couldn't believe that Aron could move at all.

"Put that down."

As quickly as Aron complied with Corin's request, Seon found himself leaning back to his side of the cab as if he'd been bitten by Corin's barked order. Aron just closed his eyes and said nothing else.

For the rest of the cab ride, Seon could not keep his eyes off the spot where he knew Aron was injured. His hands itched as if he wanted to touch it, as repulsed as he was by the very thought. The idea kept running through his head that he could help, if only he could touch that spot. It was a crazy idea, but it was in his head and he could not get it out. He had to force himself to look out the window the other way.

When the cab stopped, the trio got out in front of a highrise that was one of a thousand in the city. Corin headed into the building and Aron followed. As Seon found himself making his way to the nondescript apartment building where Aron and Corin had been staying, he found the two of them hard to believe.

He had healed the hawk because he wanted to.

Then he could heal Aron because he wanted to.

Once he had felt that power grow within himself, it awakened the desire to use it. It wasn't a one-time thing. The desire to heal was there. It was like a reminder that this was who he was meant to be. If he was going to be forced to come on this rescue mission, he might as well make himself useful.

Just as he got to the building, he heard a screech. Seon looked up and smiled. Circling overhead between the skyscrapers was the hawk. Instinctively, he held out his arm, glad he'd worn a leather jacket. The hawk landed majestically and gave his ear a gentle nip.

"Hey, girl," Seon greeted his pet. "I missed you."

Corin barely spent a glance Seon's way, and Aron seemed to hardly hang on. Seon decided that if the hawk had returned to him, it meant it was supposed to be with him. So he entered the building with the bird perched on his arm.

Fortunately, the lobby was empty. Otherwise, Seon might have gotten some strange looks for entering a twenty-first century skyscraper with a young redtail hawk on his forearm. Seon felt right at home with her there. He was right. This was where she was meant to be. For her part, she seemed perfectly content to go along for the ride. Seon entered the lift behind the others.

Corin punched in the number for an apartment on a higher floor, but it didn't take long to get there. The lift went quickly. As soon as the doors opened into the hallway leading to the apartment, Corin and Aron entered and just left the door open for Seon to follow.

The room looked completely bland. All of the rented furniture was a monochromatic dull brown. The only thing extraordinary about it was the two people occupying the space. Corin was paying attention to Aron for the first time. Aron was sitting at what was supposed to be the dining table while Corin inspected his wound. They were speaking in low voices in a language Seon couldn't make out.

Seon decided to give them some privacy, and walked over and sat on the sofa. His hands still itched to help, but he didn't dare intervene in whatever private moment they seemed to be having. It seemed more like an argument. Clearly Corin was taking Aron to task for his foolishness.

"Seon!"

Surprised at being addressed, Seon almost didn't react when Corin called his name. He jumped up and came over. Corin probably wanted his version of the story, and he found himself nervous about giving it. Aron seemed to be in enough trouble. As he was walking over, Aron asked Corin something curtly in their language.

"Did you see this?" Corin asked.

"Yes," Seon admitted. "It looks awful."

Corin didn't comment on Seon's admittedly unnecessary observation.

"Did you try anything?" Corin continued.

"What?" Seon said, not quite sure he had heard correctly. "Like what, to stop the attack?"

The look Corin sent his way told Seon what the man thought of that idea. It was admittedly not the smartest thing to say. Seon looked over at Aron, who looked a little healthier than before. There was some kind of herbal medical kit out on the table. Seon eyed it with interest.

"Did you try to heal him?" Corin clarified.

"Oh," Seon nodded. That made more sense. "I wanted to. But ... I wasn't sure if I could. I felt sort of, I don't know what ... drawn to it? The wound I mean."

It seemed best to stop stammering. Seon looked down at his hands. He felt foolish trying to explain. He wanted to help, but he had never tried to heal a person before. He didn't even know if he could.

"You are untrained, but you have healed before," Corin told him. "Let's see what you can do."

Despite the fact that Seon thought this was a terrible idea, he did as he was instructed. Carefully, he placed his hands over the area while making sure not to touch it. He could feel the warmth in his hands as an energy, almost like a buzzing. His hands wanted to heal.

Aron made a soft hissing sound, bringing Seon back to reality. His eyes popped open, and he suddenly wondered if what he was doing was hurting Aron. Corin gave him a nod, apparently to encourage continuing the process.

Focusing in on the center of the wound, Seon did his best to imagine all of his healing powers pouring into it. It didn't help that he had no idea what he was doing and was acting on instinct alone. After a while, he seemed to lose all sense of time and self. It was like he was floating in an endless bubble of warm light, with nothing there but the wound and his purpose.

Eventually he awakened, as if from a trance. He was surprised to find himself laid out on the sofa and covered in a blanket. Groggily, he sat up and looked around. The room was murkily lit with the light of twilight or early morning. There was no one else in the room. On the little table beside him he saw a hunk of bread and a stone cup of water. Once his eyes fully adjusted, he sat up and drank the water greedily. Then he collapsed back down and fell into a deep sleep.

When he woke up again, it was definitely morning. Aron was standing over him with a cocky grin, holding some kind of fruit-filled bun out over his head. Seon snorted and grabbed it, realizing as he did that his stomach was rumbling. Alix was perched on the edge of the table.

"I thought you'd never wake up," Aron said.

"What, back among the living?" Seon said between bites.

Aron shrugged, producing another roll and biting into it. "Yes. Thank you for that. What did you do?"

"I have no idea," Seon said honestly. "Corin thought I could heal you, so I did."

This was not the response that Seon wanted to give, but he had no other answers. He was watching Aron's reaction, and waiting for complaints, questions, or, knowing Aron, jokes. None came. Aron eyed Seon for a moment and then just nodded.

"He's not too happy with us, is he?" Seon said.

It wasn't really a question, but Aron's response was a curt nod. "It's me, not you, he's chuffed at," Aron said. "It was my own fault I got hurt."

As far as Seon was concerned that was a bit of an exaggeration, but he didn't say anything. He didn't know Corin well, and what he'd seen of him so far told him to steer clear of the man's temper. He decided to not mention the incident any more. It seemed less likely than ever that these two were going to let him go. Seon looked down and realized he was still wearing his school uniform and jacket, now covered in grime from yesterday's incident. Aron, on the other hand, had changed. He was now dressed in a medieval-looking tunic and trousers that seemed to be made of some kind of leather, tanned graphite gray but smooth. Corin was similarly dressed, standing behind the table in the kitchen area with a wide array of supplies. They were clearly packing to leave.

"So, you made up your mind?" Aron asked.

Corin looked up at his question and eyed Seon carefully. The expression on his face confirmed what Seon had been thinking earlier. He wondered why Aron would even ask him like he was being given a choice.

"You would let me leave?" Seon asked, aiming the question at Corin rather than Aron.

"Why don't you want to go?" Aron demanded. "Don't you see what we're up against?"

"What we're up against?" Seon said. "This has nothing to do with me. You follow me, he kidnaps me, and the next thing I know we're being shot at and I'm healing people. I'm not cut out for this."

"What makes you think that?" Corin asked in a calm voice, still not leaving the table or even interrupting his packing.

"I don't know what I'm doing, for one thing," Seon said in a voice that was as angry and disrespectful as he dared. "I tried to heal him," he pointed back to Aron, "and I passed out."

"Anyone would have," Aron said. "That was some primo work! Look."

Aron lifted up his leather tunic to show the spot that had been injured. There was still a bruise and a jagged scar, but it looked nothing like the day before. In fact, it hardly looked painful. In spite of himself, Seon gaped at it.

"What did you do?" Seon demanded, glaring at Corin.

"I simply added a paste of herbs and a tincture to what you did yesterday," Corin said. "As my apprentice says, it was fine work."

Seon sat down as Aron let go of his tunic and put his hand in his pocket again.

"Hungry?"

Without waiting for a response, Aron tossed a bun at Seon and then took another for himself. Seon could tell it wasn't his first one because Corin raised an eyebrow when his apprentice took one. Aron just shrugged though and ate the fist-sized bun in two bites. Seon sighed and ate his food more slowly, using the time to think. It was still warm and filled with something sweet that he couldn't place, with a layer of thin glaze that was both salty and sweet. He had never tasted anything like it, but it was good. He pulled off a chunk and fed it to the hawk.

"Finish packing," Corin told Aron bluntly. "I will complete Seon's kit."

"Yes, Sir," Aron replied, tossing Corin a cheeky grin and leaving the room.

Both of them seemed to have assumed that Seon was going with them. He doubted there was any way out of it at this point. Making a run for it was unlikely to get him anywhere. If he was going to do that, he should have done it last night. Seon resignedly got up and wandered over to the table to watch Corin pack. At least it looked interesting. He had never seen anything like it before.

As he watched, Seon waited expectantly for Corin to explain the strange array of items on the table. There were leather sacks in a variety of sizes, as well as jackets, pants, hats, other clothing, and some things that looked like small boxes made of wood and other materials Seon couldn't identify. He noticed more tiles like the ones Aron had showed him, as well as some rolled up objects that looked like they might be scrolls. It all seemed bizarre, but interesting. He found himself moving closer but didn't dare touch anything under Corin's stern and watchful eye.

"This will be your kit," Corin stated, pointing to a group of assembled objects separated out slightly from the others. "You have a waterskin, foodsak, assorted knives, and clothing. I have also included a rudimentary healing bag. You will build on it as we go along. I will teach you what I know, but I am not a healer. You'll learn more later when you're apprenticed, and probably learn some by instinct, unfortunately."

As the man spoke, Seon looked at the objects he was referring to. Clearly, things were a bit different wherever these two came from. Seon's world relied on technology to make everything plastic and disposable. These materials seemed like something out of a history lesson, but they also seemed more human and made to last. Seon liked them immediately. They were almost alive, as if they were calling out to him. He longed to touch them.

Seon looked up, realizing Corin was watching him. The man didn't seem unhappy to see him staring, however. On the contrary, he simply nodded.

"Go ahead and pack these," he said, gesturing toward all of the items except for the clothing, "and then get dressed in these."

He handed Seon a stack of clothing and a pair of shiny brown boots that looked heavy.

Without arguing, Seon took the clothing. He went down to the room Corin was pointing to and changed. Although the pants and tunic were made from some kind of leather, he realized that they were not stiff. The clothing was supple and somehow did not make him feel hot at all, despite being very thick. Even the jacket felt comfortable at room temperature. Seon wondered if there was some kind of magic applied to the clothing. He had no idea what the shirt was made from. It seemed to be some kind of tunic that reached almost to his knees, thin and shiny like silk. It was also a matte gray color. Best of all were the boots. They were almost solid, with no laces, and supple to the touch. They melted into his feet instantly, and did not feel nearly as heavy on his feet as they had when he was carrying them. It didn't seem like they would need any breaking in. They were already comfortable for walking in, more like running shoes than boots.

"I could get used to this," he said out loud to himself.

"Ah," Aron said from the doorway. "You like it? Expensive stuff, that. You're lucky to have that kit. It's rare."

"Yeah?" Seon asked. "Why give it to me? How is it my size?"

Aron shrugged. "Corin shrunk it last night."

Seon had no idea what that meant and decided not to ask how Corin had known his sizes. He noticed that Aron was dressed similarly, with a pack thrown over his shoulder. Unlike Seon's new-looking clothing, Aron's were covered with scars and scrapes, but still intact. Seon eyed one particularly deep gash near his left shoulder.

"You've been in some nasty fights, haven't you?"

Aron's only response was his trademark grin. Seon followed him down the hall to where Corin had finished packing everything else. The table was now empty except for three more bags. Corin picked up the two largest ones and handed one to Seon. Amazingly, it seemed to weigh almost nothing despite everything he knew was in there. Seon couldn't help peeking inside to check. The sack looked much deeper inside than it looked from the outside and everything was there. He grinned. He was definitely enjoying his first taste of magic. He could get used to this.

"You able to do this?" Aron said.

"Do I have a choice?" Seon asked.

Corin just glared at both of them, "None of us do."

Seon looked at Aron, who shrugged. Seon figured he would have to get used to Corin's enigmatic answers. In due time, he would wheedle more information out of him, or at least get it from Azoz. For now, it was time to go on an adventure.

"Alright then," Seon said. "I'm ready.

Corin just nodded and looked at Seon thoughtfully. It started to make him feel uncomfortable. He couldn't imagine what he had done wrong already.

Chapter 6

"Have you ever made yourself invisible?" Corin asked him.

"What?" Seon was so shocked his voice came out embarrassingly close to a squeak.

"Can you get people to ignore you?" Corin clarified.

"Oh," Seon said. "Maybe. They do ignore me, kinda. A lot of the time." Seon thought to himself that would explain a lot, if he was getting people to ignore him without meaning to.

Corin nodded. "I thought so. We will use that skill. Just be intentional about it. As we walk, I want you to think about how you do not want to be noticed. Try to extend it to us."

"Wow," Seon said. "Okay. I will try."

"If you don't believe you can do it, it will not work," Corin said firmly, as if that was all there was to it. "Just believe it, and it will work."

Seon nodded, determined to succeed in this small task. Corin seemed unyielding and he wanted to get off to a good start. Azoz didn't seem to mind the man's demeanor, but he made Seon uncomfortable. He knew that he would end up on his bad side eventually, even though Seon considered himself generally a good kid. Corin just seemed like the kind that didn't have a good side.

As they headed toward the door, Seon held out his arm, but the hawk landed on his hat. Seon shrugged and exchanged grins with Aron. He tried not to look at Corin.

The group walked out and down the door. It clicked to lock behind them. In the lift, no one said a word. As soon as they entered the lobby below, Seon lowered his eyelids almost closed and began concentrating on making the people around him ignore the strangely dressed trio and hawk. No one looked their way. It was working.

There was a cab waiting when they reached the front of the building. The three of them got in wordlessly, along with Seon's hawk. The driver seemed to know where to go already. As soon as the three of them were seated, he set off. The driver paid no attention to them, but Seon kept up the avoidance intention and they were still ignored. Seon looked out the window. He had no idea where they were going. After the medieval gear-up, getting in a cab seemed a strange way to begin a trip.

The car dropped them off at the entrance to what looked like a national park. Seon couldn't see the sign, but they were definitely in a nature preserve. The hawk took flight, circling lazily ahead of them. Seon watched her appreciatively.

As if by magic or instinct or both, the hawk came fluttering instantly down to Seon's arm. It was infinitely more comfortable with his new jacket. He didn't feel a thing.

"Whoa," Aron tutted. "You have her trained already?"

"Not exactly," Seon admitted. "I just *wanted* her to come, so she did."

Aron nodded. "That's your Gift."

"I'm using magic?" Seon asked with a frown, unsure how he could be using magic without knowing it. He gestured, and Alix flew off again, resuming her lazy circling.

"Your people call it magic," Aron said, with a touch of scorn in his voice. "*Magic* is showing off, like playing a trick. What you're doing is *intention*."

"What's the difference?" Seon asked, both confused and curious now. He could see Corin far in the distance from them, what seemed too far away to listen.

"It's all the difference," Azoz explained. "Magic has no purpose but to entertain. What we do is not magic in your world. We do not put on shows or do tricks. We are using our Gifts for real things. It can be the difference between life and death."

"I've seen you play around with your Gifts," Seon commented.

He was sure that he had now that he thought back. Aron had manipulated tablets and screens in classrooms, messed with people's watches, and even locked and unlocked doors as pranks. There was no way that Aron could claim that any of these things were done for any purpose other than to create chaos or amuse himself.

"Well," Aron looked ahead, where Corin was still walking nowhere near them. "Occasionally, I have done some things I'm not proud of."

Seon glared at him. He had a feeling that Aron was proud of most of them.

Corin turned around, and Seon could see the glare he sent Aron even from as far away as they were. It seemed to have only a slight dampening effect. The only response it got was for Aron to speed up slightly and send some kind of gesture back at Corin that Seon couldn't interpret, putting his fist to his forehead. It might have been anything from a salute to an agreement to hurry up and stop fooling around.

"You like to push things, don't you?" Seon asked coolly.

"Sure," Aron replied. "Why not?"

"Because he doesn't seem at all happy with us, that's why," Seon said. "Or with you."

"Why do you care?" Aron asked, raising an eyebrow in an almost exact imitation of the gesture Corin had just made to him.

"He doesn't seem like the sort to let things slide, that's why," Seon said. "He'll just as likely take it out on me."

Aron stopped walking and gave Seon a long appraising look. "You have nothing to worry about, " he said finally, and then continued walking.

"I don't," Seon asked. "Why not?"

"He's not your mentor," Aron replied bluntly.

"So?" Seon pressed. "He's in charge. I'm on this mission too, against my will I might add. He could do anything to me. So could you. The two of you could kill me and bury me in these woods and no one would ever know what happened to me."

Aron looked at Seon with a dead-eyed expression and then burst out laughing. "That's a good one," he said with a crowing laugh.

"What's so funny?" Seon demanded. The boys were no longer walking.

"You're one of the Gifted," Aron said. "Do you know how few of us there are? You are also the first Gifted to be identified in Modicus for over a thousand years. Your presence was foretold. The Domium would love to get their hands on you. We are *protecting* you. Why would we kill you?"

All Seon could do was stare at his friend. He hadn't understood half of what Aron had just said. What he had understood did not sound good. He wasn't sure if it made him want to turn around and leave or stick closer to these people. It certainly sounded like he needed their protection. He finally settled for asking a question.

"How do you know all this?"

Aron's cool demeanor finally seemed to slip for the briefest time. Then his easy grin returned. "Corin told me some. Some of it is just well-known. I picked up the rest."

With that puzzling statement, Azoz started walking, hurrying to catch up with Corin. Seon frowned, more annoyed than ever. The whole thing was making less and less sense.

"What do you mean, you 'picked it up?' And what part is 'well-known?' Who knows it? I don't," Seon stalked after Aron, practically shouting in his annoyance. "Hey. Answer me."

Reaching out to grab Aron's arm, Seon found himself flat on his back instead. He looked up to see the boy staring down at him with a grin. Seon did not grin back.

"Don't take it personally. No one tells me everything either," he said. He then held out his hand to help Seon up.

Reluctantly, Seon took the proffered hand with a grimace. He had landed hard on his back. By the expression on his face, Aron thought the whole thing was hilarious. Seon watched thoughtfully as Aron trotted away at an easy clip. He was a very strange kid. They both were strange. Seon was beginning to wonder what he had gotten into. He had just met them, and without much thought he had agreed to take off on a journey to a mysterious other dimension with them to find (not rescue) a girl he didn't even know based on only a dream. The more he thought about all of this, it was starting to seem like one long nightmare. Maybe he had accidentally ingested a plant with psychotropic properties. His imagination wasn't good enough to come up with all of this on his own.

After what seemed like miles of walking, Aron stopped. Seon realized it was because Corin had stopped. As far as Seon could see, there was no reason to stop. Soon, they were all three stopped … nowhere. Seon waited expectantly for the reason to make itself apparent.

"This is not going to be an easy journey," Corin said. "You will be tested in ways I can't explain to you now, because I do not know myself. I am not a Seer. Know that if you do follow this path, you will learn much about yourself, and grow in ways you never would otherwise."

Seon let that sink in. He figured the path Corin described was metaphorical. They were on a trail that was not well-marked, but Corin and Aron seemed to be able to follow it. Seon was just following them.

"You would let me go?" Seon asked. Then he shook his head. "I guess not. I need to go, anyway, even if I do not have a choice. This is something I am supposed to do. I know I am no hero."

Corin gave him a funny look, but did not answer. He hadn't said anything about letting Seon go, after all. It was more like he was telling him not to mess up. Seon sighed.

"Look, I get it. You aren't going to let me go. It's not like I could get away from the two of you anyway. I'll try not to mess this up too badly," Seon said.

"Very well," Corin said. Then he turned and kept walking.

Aron cocked an eyebrow at Seon and then followed Corin. With a small sigh, Seon stayed there for a few minutes, wondering if he had made the right decision or if he should have tried to fight. Then he thought of the girl in his dreams and he too continued down the trail.

Seon followed Aron at a slight distance. There was silence for a time. So long passed without talking that Seon began to wonder how far they were going to walk. Curiosity began to get the better of him.

"Where are we going?"

No one answered. Seon didn't say anything else. He found the silence unnerving. Eventually, he reached into his sack for the waterskin and drank. He noticed that Corin and Aron occasionally took a drink from theirs, but they hadn't suggested it yet. He was getting thirsty. The water was cool and felt good on his throat.

It felt like they went on for miles like that, in perfect silence. Aron was a few steps away from Corin now, and Seon was a few steps from him. The journey was so monotonous that Seon was beginning to get sleepy. He barely had time to think that was strange, that he was sleepy while walking, when they came to a structure. It looked like a large pyramid overgrown with vines and moss. He figured it was either a service building or an entertainment venue for the park.

Seon barely heard Corin speak to Aron from the edges of his consciousness as they entered the building. He didn't even remember seeing a door. Before he knew it, they were somewhere much cooler. He might have closed his eyes, just for a minute. When he opened them, he was outside again.

He was also in a completely different place.

The weather was different. It had been a sunny, clear day—neither hot nor cold. Now it was overcast, threatening rain any second. Seon looked around. He had been sleepy before, but now he was instantly alert. Panicked, he whistled. A screech answered him. Seon felt awash with relief.

"Don't worry, she's here," Aron said from somewhere behind him.

Seon had no time for Aron right now. He could feel something in the air around him, and it wasn't the storm. There was a threat, imminent. Judging by Alix's stance on his shoulder, she felt it too. He could sense her thoughts. They weren't clear like a human's words would be, but she definitely knew danger was near.

"What is it?" Aron asked. For the first time since Seon had known him, his voice did not seem light. He was worried.

"I don't know what they are," Seon admitted, closing his eyes to try to get a better fix on the threat. "There's a lot of them."

"There's a storm coming," Aron said, looking around as if he could feel something Seon could not see.

Seon looked at him and tried to avoid responding to that with a snort. Any fool could see that this was no storm. Something else was coming. It was coming fast, using the storm as cover.

The three looked around. The pyramid was behind them, with walls of solid stone. It provided no shelter from either the sleet that was beginning to fall or threats of any kind. There was a forest in the distance. It was too far to make, even in a fast run. The only option was to fight.

Chapter 7

It was clear that Corin was deliberating on their options. Seon had no training and only rudimentary magic. Aron clearly had been trained to fight. Seon knew that from seeing him in action. His Gift of manipulating energy would not be much use here. That was what Seon thought at first. Then he saw Aron looking up.

"Now way," he breathed. "Are you serious?"

As the storm increased, bolts of lightning were charging through the sky, increasing in intensity with each round. Seon looked at them incredulously. He had no idea what Aron was planning to do with that lightning, and he didn't want to be anywhere near him when he did it.

"Whatever's coming is alive," he said to them. "I can manipulate them. I've done it before."

He tried to sound confident in that statement, even though he was shivering from the cold as the rain drenched his face. The jacket and pants protected the rest of his body, and he was surprisingly warm. It might not have all been cold making him shake. The words were mostly exaggeration and half-truths. He had never done anything of the sort. The most he'd done was half-heartedly participate in some of Aron's whole-class opranks. He'd made a hedgehog dance and told a snake to chase some boys down a hallway. This was nothing like that.

Corin probably knew that, but there was no choice. The three of them made a triangle, backs to one another, and then spread out. Aron's face was pure determination. Seon was pretty sure his looked like he was about to sick up. Corin's was a blank, as always.

Since he had a task to do and not much time to do it in, Seon closed his eyes and focused in on the life forms that were headed that way. They were small, but many. He had no idea what that meant, and if it was a good thing or a bad thing. On his shoulder, Alix was trembling in excitement, ready to fight. In concentration, Seon found himself almost linking with her consciousness. He focused in and realized what it was.

Birds. They were birds.

Just in time, he looked up. Flying in their direction, above them, swarming near the ground at their feet, and flying in circles all around them, were thousands of green-orange colored crows. These crows were like none Seon had ever seen before. They were the size of geese and twice as mean. When they came near him, he could see their beady red eyes. Somehow, those eyes seemed sightless, as if they were being directed by an outside force.

Ignoring the ghastly image, Seon closed his eyes and focused on gaining control of the beasts, wrenching it away from whoever was manipulating them. They were not individually minded. They seemed to have a hive mind, and Seon had no idea where it was. He forced himself into the hive mind, feeling his way around for the one in control. As he did so, he could feel the presence of Alix, fighting them off. He could tell when she was pecked or rolled, he saw every injury she sustained, even with his eyes closed. He saw it in his very soul.

Seon wasn't coming away unscathed either. The crows were targeting him, either because he was there, or because they knew he was trying to attack them. He should not have seemed like a threat, just standing there with his eyes closed. The birds certainly saw him as one though. They were on him everywhere, pecking at his face and hands until he was raw and bloody. Seon wasn't sure if there were gloves in his kit, but he was wishing he had put them on. Still, he ignored the birds and focused on his task. He knew the others were also being viscously attacked by the crows and also ignoring them.

On the periphery of his vision, he could tell that Corin and Azoz were not idle. Aron was manipulating the lightning. Somewhere in the back of his mind, Seon spared a thought for wishing that he could open his eyes and see it for himself. He saw it only through the terror of the hive mind, for there was fire in the air, and it was being directed at them. It was taking them out by the dozens, singeing them all at once—their hearts to beat no more.

Meanwhile, Corin had an equally valuable talent. He grasped the birds right from the air without touching them. He just reached up with the wind and pulled them down. The sheer force of his grasp shattered them from the inside out. Although he could often take no more than two or three of them at a time, he often dashed birds against each other in doing so, or smashed them against rocks or trees. He was racking up quite a number of kills at this rate. Still, that seemed not to be enough for him, so he tossed a great boulder into the sky, taking three dozen crows at once.

By this point, Seon had finally gotten control of the hive mind, with Alix's help. He convinced it that these travelers were too dangerous, and the murder should leave. It was not a difficult argument to make by that point. Their numbers had been greatly reduced. Just minutes after the fighting had started, the birds took flight and left through the storm. It was over.

Seon collapsed into the muddy ground, exhausted from his efforts. He felt as if the life was drained out of him. Somehow, he knew that he should see to the others, but he didn't have any strength left in him to do it. Alix landed next to him, hopping along on bloody feet. One of her wings seemed to be broken and her beak was cracked. Feeling close to tears, Seon reached out to lay his hand over her soothingly. It was the last thing he remembered before losing consciousness.

"Seon. Seon!"

Seon opened a groggy eye. Aron was holding a clay mug of some kind of tea in front of his nose. He held out his hand, even though he wasn't sure he could grasp it. He was surprised to see that his hand seemed almost completely healed. Startled, he looked around.

"Where's Alix?" he croaked.

"Hunting, I think," Aron said.

Now that Seon could see his face better, Azoz looked terrible. His skin was pale and chalky, so that the veins were clearly visible. He had paste lathered all over his cheeks and hands as well.

Aron saw Seon looking at his hands and held them up. "Corin's been at me from the healer's bag," he said wryly. "The lighnting did a number on my skin. Dried it out. I'm alive though. We're all alive."

"Didn't you get pecked?" Seon asked?

"Well, sure, some of them tried," Aron said with a harsh laugh. "They got fried pretty quickly if they did though. I was totally electrified."

Seon smiled at the image and shook his head. He had no idea what that must have been like. He'd seen Aron manipulate energy before, but nothing like that. He was surprised the boy was still alive.

"Are you okay though?"

"Sure, nothing a few weeks' rest wouldn't cure," Aron joked. "We're leaving in the morning though."

Seon smirked to match Aron's expression. He was beginning to wonder at his friend's sense of humor. At least nothing ever seemed to get him down. Seon looked at his own hands, wondering what had happened.

"What about me?" he asked. "The healer's bag?"

"No," Aron said slowly. "I guess he didn't need to."

"What do you mean?" Seon said, confused.

"You healed yourself," Aron shrugged. "Alix is fine. You healed her too."

Seon didn't respond. All he remembered was falling asleep, or unconscious, with his hand on Alix. He must have healed her and himself during that time. He was a little disturbed by that. If he was going to be doing something magical, he wanted to know he was doing it and be in control.

"You should eat something," Aron said, as if he had just thought of it. "Corin's out. He left some rations."

Aron walked over to a log, where there was a sort of leather pot. That was the best way Seon could describe it. It was hanging over a fire. Seon had no idea how the pot worked but was too tired to care. Aron pulled another stone mug out of a sak and scooped it into the pot, then brought it to Seon.

"Drink up," he said. "It's a sort of stew. Corin said you should find us some legumes and roots and stuff, once you're on your feet."

Seon nodded. He had been on hikes in nature reserves a few times. It was one of the few activities he enjoyed with his older brothers. He'd always had a gift for finding edible plants. Now, he realized, it probably was an actual Gift. At least there was something he could do to make himself useful for the group.

The stew was excellent. It was seasoned with herbs that Seon suspected had healing properties. It made him feel better almost instantly, and not just because he was so hungry. It was more filling than the small serving should have been, and it tasted delicious. The stew was savory with just a touch of spiciness. Seon didn't think he had ever tasted anything better in his life. It was hardly what he would expect from trail food.

As soon as he finished, he returned the mug to Aron. The two boys went up to the edge of the clearing where they were camping. Seon could already see a few bushes of berries that looked edible back in the thicket. He was eager to go make himself useful. While Aron stayed behind, Seon used one of his empty saks to gather berries, herbs, a kind of tuber that looked something like a potato, and mushrooms that he sensed would be safe to eat.

When he had been gone about an hour, he decided it was a good idea to return. The sak was nowhere near full, even though when he held it up it didn't seem that large. It must have been somehow larger on the inside than the outside. Seon decided not to question it, since everything else that had happened to him lately was unexplainable based on his usual standards. He walked carefully back to their base, wary of predators since it was now getting later in the day, based on the sun's position.

By the time he arrived at their camp, Corin had returned. Without a word, Seon handed him the sak containing what he had found. He found himself strangely nervous, as if he wanted to please the others. Corin looked inside the sak and handed it to Aron, who closed it by cinching the leather string. Even though neither of them said anything, Seon felt oddly relieved.

"Since it's nearly dark, we'll sleep here tonight," Corin said. "Get some sleep."

Aron nodded. Corin walked off, leaving Seon feeling confused. He looked to Aron, who gestured for him to follow. He led them to a corner by the fire where Aron had prepared the ground, clearing away the rocks. It wasn't cold, but Seon was grateful for the fire. It would keep away larger predators and make the area cheerier. Corin's taciturn nature and Aron's general lack of information were beginning to get to Seon.

Despite his frustration, Seon was tired. He took the blanket that Aron handed him and went to the edge of the clearing wordlessly. It looked thin, but after he spread it on the ground and got himself stretched out on it, he couldn't feel the ground beneath him. A thick mattress wouldn't have been any better. Despite the day's dramatic events, he felt himself drifting off to sleep as if on a cloud.

It felt like no time had passed when he awoke the next morning to the sounds of clattering. Aron was standing over him, stirring one of the same mug-like cups Seon had used the night before with some kind of metal rod. His presence so close roused Seon to consciousness quickly, though he wasn't sure why Azoz standing over him like that should make him uncomfortable.

"Sorry," he mumbled. "Did I oversleep?"

Either the question or the attitude seemed to amuse Aron, but he said nothing and simply held out the mug. Seon frowned. There wasn't really much to get ready, since he had slept in the same clothes as he'd worn yesterday, but he didn't like being behind. He was already enough out of the loop.

Aron walked away, and Seon drank the substance in the cup. It was thicker than the substance from the night before—more like a spicy porridge. Seon had never appreciated porridge much, but he was hungry, and it tasted good. He idly wondered if it was from rations they had brought with them. In all of the activity, he'd not had time to inspect his kit. He idly wondered if there was something in there to brush his teeth. He hadn't done so last night, and though he doubted hygiene would be a top priority on a journey such as this, he couldn't imagine going much longer without doing something about it.

Fully awake now, Seon realized that he hadn't seen Alix yet. He whistled, and in less than a minute, she was on his arm. She must have been perched nearby. He stroked her tail feathers soothingly while she nipped at his hair gently.

After finishing the meager but surprisingly filling breakfast, Seon brought Azoz the mug and decided to bring up housekeeping. "Say, how do you clean this?" he asked. "And what about us? I don't suppose we packed toothbrushes?"

"This is easy," Aron said, taking the mug. He tossed a powder that looked like sand inside and held it to the fire. There was a splash of flame and then he handed it back to Seon, who took it carefully. It was completely cool to the touch.

"Wow," Seon nodded, impressed.

At this, Aron shrugged. Clearly whatever magic he'd just done to clean the mug was no big deal to him. "It's just a simple spell. As for the toothbrush...." Aron reached inside a small pouch and handed Seon a leaf. "Chew this."

Seon took the leaf and sniffed it appraisingly. "Mint?" He chewed it for a few minutes. The leaf foamed and disappeared. It did not taste exactly like toothpaste, of course, or like any mint leaves he had ever chewed. His mouth felt fresh and clean, and so did his teeth.

"That's amazing."

Aron just grinned. "You forget, I did spend some time among your people. I know what a toothbrush is. This is similar."

"A spell too?" Seon asked, curious as to what had caused the effect.

"Not exactly," Aron said. "It's an herb that grows naturally. It's just been ... enhanced."

Seon nodded. He could see how that would work. He suddenly found his mind whirring with possibilities. This was something he could do. He knew it. He didn't know how yet, but he knew that it was in him, just waiting to come out.

"Yeah, well, we need to get going," Aron said. "The sun is already up. We're supposed to forage more. I can show you what I know, and you're supposed to see what you can find. With your Gift."

"Where's Corin?"

"Around."

Seon frowned. It seemed like Corin was gone more than he was there. Seon wasn't sure how he felt about that. Corin wasn't especially good company, and in some ways Seon was relieved that the dour man wasn't there to watch him constantly and find fault. Seon still had no idea what to expect from him. They were just kids though, and Corin was their leader. It didn't seem like they'd made much progress so far and all Seon had been told to do was wander around and try to 'use' his Gift, with no direction whatsoever on how to do that. He'd had more help from Aron than Corin, and Aron was just as mysterious and definitely more annoying with his smirks and lack of detail.

Since there wasn't much Seon could do about any of it, he just hiked his sak onto his shoulder and started walking in the direction his senses were vaguely directing him. Aron followed with no comment. The boots were comfortable, and oddly enough left no footprints. Just another strange facet of this unusual world. Seon noticed but said nothing. He had decided it was better to ask fewer questions, since he was getting few answers.

They were going in the opposite direction from his previous day's foraging. Alix flew in her characteristic lazy circles about their heads. After about ten minutes of walking, they came to a clearing with a stream and a huge berry patch. Alix eagerly pecked at a berry. Even if Seon hadn't known it intuitively, that confirmed that they were safe to eat.

"Do you know how to weave a basket?" Seon asked.

"What good would that do?" Azoz asked. "We can't really carry it?"

Seon looked at the berry patch. Azoz was probably right. The berries wouldn't keep, and would get squished in their saks. He looked at the sun, and then at Azoz. It was his turn to smirk.

"We could dry them."

Azoz returned the smirk. Seon could almost see his thought process go from doubtful to excited.

"Let's do it!"

Using the same sand-fire process as before, Aron cleaned off a rock by the stream while Seon made a basket from dried reeds and then filled it with berries. He laid the berries out in a single layer and stepped back, looking at Aron. He honestly wasn't sure if this was going to work. If it did, he had no idea how Corin would react. Chances were good they were both going to be in huge trouble. Still, it might just be worth it to see if Aron could dry the berries without completely scorching them.

Seon stepped way back. He had seen Aron control lightning, but he didn't want to be anywhere near those berries. He watched in fascination while Azoz held his hand out. At first, nothing happened. Then a streak of light flashed from the sky and hit the rock with an enormous crash, breaking it in two. Alix squawked, annoyed.

Aron stepped back, and then looked over to Seon with chagrin.

"Whoops," he said. "Too much power, I guess."

Seon walked over to the rock. It was singed black and cleaved in two. There was no sign of the berries other than a splash of red like blood over most of its surface.

"Hmm," Seon said. "Okay, harnessing the power of the sun to dry out berries might not have been my best idea."

Aron laughed, a short, honest laugh. Clearly, he wasn't disappointed by his failure. Seon noted that Azoz didn't get upset by much. He took most things in stride, unlike Seon.

"You know," Aron said, giving Seon a meaningful look. "I think you might be better for this."

"What?" Seon scoffed. "How?"

"You manipulate plants, right?" Aron said. "When plants die, they shrivel up. Including the fruit."

Seon just looked at Aron. It was something Seon probably should have thought of himself. In hindsight, it made perfect sense. It was worth a try.

"Let's get more berries."

After Seon and Aron had collected more berries, and found and cleaned off another rock, Seon sat cross-legged in front of the rock trying to concentrate. In his mind, he tried to picture the berries as dried up. He focused on that for several long minutes, then opened his eyes. The berries remained as plump and juicy as ever. Seon tossed one to Alix in irritation. She caught it in midair.

"No?" Aron asked.

"It's no use," Seon complained. "I can't do it."

"What happens to them? How do they become dried?"

It was a simple question. Seon thought about how he communicated with Alix, or the way he worked with his plants. It was all about the innate nature of the organism. He would have to do that with the berries. He was going about this the wrong way. Closing his eyes, he pictured the life cycle of the plant, and the purpose of the berry in that cycle. He pictured the berry dying, shriveling up, disconnected from its life source on the plant. Then he opened his eyes.

The berries were all completely dried out.

"I did it," he breathed.

"You did," Aron said. "How about that?"

Seon picked up one of the shriveled berries and looked at it in awe. This wasn't just some magic trick he had just performed. It was part of their survival. The berries were a food source, and rich in antioxidants. He popped it in his mouth. They also tasted delicious.

"Time to go back," Aron said suddenly.

"What?" Seon asked. "Why? All we have is the berries."

"Corin wants us to," he said simply.

Figuring it was some kind of mentor-apprentice connection, Seon decided not to ask how Aron knew that. He just followed as Azoz led them back toward the camp by a route that seemed much faster than the one they had taken to get to the stream. That suited Seon fine. He felt tired, and he wondered if it had something to do with the berries.

As they walked, Seon realized that Aron wasn't all bad. After all, he could even sometimes be helpful. He watched Aron thoughtfully as they walked back.

"Hey," Seon said. "I'm sorry if I've been kind of a pain. I guess I need to take this thing more seriously. I kind of resented being forced into it, and not being told anything much. Or anything at all, really."

Aron gave him his signature half-smile and didn't respond.

"Maybe we should start over," Seon said, stopping dead. "I'm serious. Hello, my name is Seon." Seon held out a hand, as if to shake Aron's.

Raising one eyebrow, Aron stopped and looked at Seon. Then he held out his own hand. "Hello, my name is Azoz."

"What?"

It was Seon's turn to laugh. In hindsight, it made perfect sense that Aron, or Azoz, would make up a name to fit in undercover. He did not know whether to keep laughing or be annoyed.

"And Corin's name is?" Seon demanded.

"Oh, that's his name," Azoz shrugged.

"What else aren't you telling me?" Seon asked.

Azoz just smirked and did not reply. Seon knew that there wasn't a way he was going to get any more out of him. He gave up and continued on after him, shaking his head at the new development. There was definitely more that they were not telling him.

When they arrived back at the camp, Corin was indeed waiting. He didn't seem annoyed, so they must not have been late. When Azoz made no excuses or explanations about where they were, Seon started to wonder if it was his role to explain what they had been doing.

"Um, we found some berries," he began tentatively. "Since berries aren't likely to keep long or very well, I, uh, I dried them out."

Seon felt very fidgety as he made this report. He wasn't sure why, exactly. He didn't think he had been doing anything wrong, but he wasn't entirely sure he was allowed to be doing it either. Corin was a complete mystery to him and staring into the man's blank expression as he explained was not helping matters. Azoz also said nothing. Seon felt that he should be getting a little help from Azoz, since he was Corin's apprentice.

"I see."

Not sure what to say to that, Seon looked to Azoz and raised an eyebrow in the universally understood plea for assistance. Azoz was standing stock still and saying nothing, but Corin was looking at him, not Seon. For all Seon knew, they were using telepathy.

"Well, Azoz, he said ...," Seon tried not to sound nervous. "He said I was supposed to be using my Gift. To forage."

Corin inclined his head slightly, not reacting at all to the fact that Seon had used Azoz's real name. For whatever reason, Azoz decided to speak. Seon felt relieved that at least one of them was.

"He found berries, obviously, and they're edible, but it took some time to figure out how to dry them."

So that was it. Seon found himself rather miffed that Corin was annoyed that they had only found berries when he thought it rather clever to dry the berries. Berries were a healthy food and tasty too. Corin was entirely too picky. Seon frowned.

"Very well," Corin said. "We will set out now. Everything is packed up already."

Azoz nodded, and Corin walked off. Seon waited until Corin had walked some distance, and then turned to Azoz in a huff.

"What, that's it?"

Azoz shrugged.

"What was that all about, anyway? I was supposed to capture, kill, and dress some large animal in the past two hours?" Seon asked Azoz.

A small smile passed Azoz's lips at that image. "Look, that's just the way he is, okay. Don't let it get to you."

"Are we in trouble?" Seon demanded as they began to walk. "Did we almost get in trouble? Should I not have done what I did?"

"Look," Azoz said. "Don't worry about it."

"Don't worry about what. Which part?" Seon persisted.

Azoz didn't respond. They kept walking. Seon went over the exchange in his head a few more times over the next few hours and finally gave it up. He wasn't sure he would ever figure these two out.

Not an athlete by any means, Seon had never considered himself in poor shape. How Azoz and Corin could march along at a constant pace through rugged terrain that would make most armies jealous was beyond him. The sun was high in the sky now as well. The hat he'd been issued kept it out of his eyes and there was a bandana-type cloth that kept his neck cool, but Seon was miserable. Alix seemed fine, although she did occasionally take breaks from her flying to perch on his hat.

The sun was setting by the time they began to slow down. At first, Seon thought Corin was starting to tire of the relentless pace. Then he realized that their leader had just been looking for a spot to camp. Azoz was also on the lookout, but no one had let Seon in on the secret. He realized this when Azoz trotted up to Corin and said something to him. Corin gave a sharp nod and Azoz stopped, waiting for Seon to catch up.

"We're stopping here for the night," Azoz said.

Seon heard a note of pride in his voice. He understood why when they got to the spot. Corin was already setting up the cookstand and the strange cooking sak.

"Well spotted," he said to Azoz. "There's a creek down there."

Azoz nodded and gestured for Seon to follow. Seon had to hurry to catch up. Somehow Azoz had the energy to jog down to the water. Where he got it from was a complete mystery to Seon.

"You got to choose the spot, huh?" Seon asked, catching his breath as he plopped down next to Azoz on the bank.

"Yup."

Azoz was pulling off his boots, and Seon suddenly understood his excitement. He had his boots off almost as fast. Minutes later, both boys were in the creek splashing each other. Even Alix was on the bank, hopping around from rock to rock in the shallow part of the water.

"Wow, this feels good," Seon breathed. "Why didn't we do this earlier?"

"We were too distracted frying berries," Azoz said, filling his hat with water and dumping it on Seon's head.

After a while, Corin joined them. They cooled off in the stream and Corin filled the waterskins. Seon could have sworn the man even smiled, but it might have been his imagination. When they'd had their fill of fun, they returned to the camp exhausted and dried out by the fire. Corin came back a while later with a basket full of fish. They tasted delicious, even though normally Seon avoided eating anything that once moved.

After they ate, Corin and Azoz did the cleaning up, since it seemed to take skills Seon didn't have yet. That suited Seon fine tonight. He was feeling sleepy from a full belly and the long journey. At this point, he was ready to pull out his blanket and go to sleep, but he noticed that Azoz and Corin didn't seem to be preparing to sleep, so he didn't. He was following their lead. It was during these times that Seon often tried to ask questions.

"What's with that crystal you carry with you?" Seon asked Azoz as they sat.

The crystal was light purple, almost fuschia. He had seen Azoz carry it around in a pouch or place it inside a decorative metal casing he wore around his neck, shaped in a spiral on a leather cord. The times when it was out were few, so Seon would hardly have noticed it if Azoz did not seem to be almost secretive about having it out. It must have been important. If Corin had something similar, Seon had never seen it. Corin did have a similar medallion though.

"It's my clan *indicum*," Azoz said, pulling it out of its hiding place and holding it up to the light. "It's an amethyst, for Clan Amethyst. I guess you will be Clan Amethyst too, when you begin your training. When you become an apprentice."

"Where did you get it?" Seon asked.

"They are passed down, sometimes, in families. Or sometimes you find them, during a trial. This one was passed down to me," Azoz said, running his fingers over the crystal's smooth surface.

"What does it do?" Seon asked. He could feel energy radiating from the stone, and something else. It was almost as if it spoke to him, without using words. As if it was alive, in some immortal, non-sentient way.

"Many things," Azoz's voice was soft, as if he was speaking from far away. "You can use them to focus meditation. To call members of your can. Even to store energy."

Seon was impressed. He wouldn't think a small stone the size of a coin could do all that, if he was not able to feel the energy radiating off of this one. From that, he could start to believe it.

"How?" Seon asked.

"It's a spell," Azoz said with a shrug. "And it's your Clan's stone, so you're in tune to it."

"Oh," Seon said, not really understanding at all. "I could probably use something like that."

"Not likely," Azoz said with a scoff. "You are nowhere near ready."

Seon nodded, trying not to be offended. He had to admit that his powers were raw and untamed. Even if he had such a stone, he would not know what to do with it.

"I don't have a clan, anyway," Seon said.

"You do," Azoz said. "You're Amethyst, like us."

"How do you know?" Seon asked.

"We would not be able to find you otherwise," Azoz said, as if that explained everything.

Seon thought about that for a while. It did make sense. He had wondered how they had known where he was and where to look for him. Azoz did not seem inclined to continue with the matter, so Seon moved on to another.

"So, where are we headed, anyway?"

Corin looked up. He had stayed out of the other conversation. For a moment, he didn't say anything. He seemed to be weighing how much to say or when to say it. Apparently, he decided to was okay to start telling Seon *something*.

"We are headed to the magical capital of Medeis. In Home World, which is what we call this land, also known as Domium, there are many dialects for different regions, including Conlatian for the region we are walking through now. You are aware that the Umbra, "Shadow Men" as they are called, lurk in every village and in between, and we must be on the lookout for them, as they are on the lookout for us. That is all I will say about that for now."

Seon really wanted to know more about that subject, but the look on Corin's face told him that it was closed, so when Corin paused, Seon took the moment to ask Azoz a question.

"How many languages do you speak?"

On this note, Seon was feeling a little inferior. He only spoke his own language. In school they had tried to teach him a second language and he had learned a few basic phrases and words in a couple of years. Azoz just smirked playfully. Seon knew that Azoz spoke at least two languages. He spoke Seon's language and his own.

"It is not important now," Corin said dismissively. "You'll pick it up. We will teach you basic dialects, but your language is spoken here since travel through the portals is common this close. Most dialects are evolved from Latin. Surely, they taught that to you at that school, at least as a so-called 'dead' or root language?"

Seon just shook his head. He knew some Greek and Latin roots, but that was about it. Corin scoffed and muttered something that sounded vaguely familiar, or like it should be familiar. Azoz looked like he was trying not to laugh.

"No matter," Corin said. "You are aware of what our mission is. We will continue your training. Most of the journey will be as today. We will engage in hunting and foraging for food. You will be our main source of food. Azoz and I have other responsibilities. Since your Gifts are in those areas, you can be the most use there. I will train you when I can, and so will Azoz."

"Wait, wait?"

There were so many things wrong with that proclamation that Seon wasn't sure where to begin. He took a deep breath, not wanting to be difficult or bring Corin's wrath down on his head. The man was already glowering at him. He knew he was speaking out of turn, but he had to say something. He started with the obvious first.

"Azoz will train me?" Seon didn't bother pointing out that he and Azoz seemed close to the same age.

"Certainly," Corin responded as if talking to a small child. "Azoz has been my apprentice for several years and has other training that you do not have before that. He can train you in the basics that you also do not have, being not from our world. Cultural aspects will be foreign to you. At this point, you might make a mistake in a village and get yourself and one of us killed. To avoid you dooming this mission to failure before it begins,

Azoz will acquaint you with basic rural customs and protocol as well as dangers you will be unaware of. I suggest you get used to that. There is no room for childish pride here. This is serious. Can you accept that, or can't you? If you can't, you should never have come."

"Yes, sir," Seon said, swallowing heavily. He couldn't even look at Azoz. "I mean, I can."

"What is your other objection?"

For a moment, Seon couldn't even remember what it was. Corin's lecture was ringing in his ears. Then it hit him. He wasn't sure if he could bring it up. He had to, somehow. His conscience was prickling him.

"Well, you see ... I can find herbs, and edible plants, that's easy enough. It's just that ...." Seon found himself unable to continue.

Corin fixed him with a firm glare. "You can, and will, hunt. Protein is necessary for sustenance. We cannot survive on roots and berries. Are you saying that you are a vegetarian?"

Seon nodded. So far, it hadn't been an issue. He hadn't even thought about what had been in the stew the night before. It was better not to ask sometimes.

"Out of the question," Corin insisted. "You will have to find a way around it."

"But ... I can feel them, Sir," Seon said, trying not to sound like a whiny child. He was desperately trying to explain. "I know what they are feeling."

"I understand," Corin said, firmly but without malice. "They are not sentient beings, Seon. They are animals. You feel a connection with your familiar. She exists to you on a higher level, because you have connected to her. She is still not a sentient, as you and I are. If you like, you can connect to the animals and get them to willingly give themselves up to you. Find the oldest and the weakest. We cannot eat any diseased, however. And the oldest do not give the best meat. It is not the best solution."

Seon felt frustrated. He didn't like that suggestion at all.

"Seon," Azoz said suddenly. "Think about what you did with the berries. The life cycle? Animals prey on other animals. The strong prey on the weak. We are strong. We are just preying on weaker animals."

"Are you suggesting we just stick to smaller animals?" Seon demanded.

"If you insist," Corin said, with what almost sounded like resignation in his voice. "They are certainly easier to prepare for cooking."

Seon nodded. He didn't like it at all, but he could see their point. He hated this part of his job, but he understood why they had given it to him.

"How about a compromise," Azoz said. "You lure them in, and I'll kill them."

"What?" Seon asked. "Fry their brains or something?"

"Zap them. Quick, painless death. I'll even do the preparing for you. I'm good at it. Corin always makes me do the grunt work." Azoz shot Corin a crooked grin.

"Okay," Seon said, to stop the discussion if nothing else.

"Fine," Corin said. "I do not care. Just get it done."

Seon rubbed his hand along the back of his neck. He was beginning to realize that parts of this journey would be very difficult. He looked up at Azoz, who gave him a reassuring nod. Corin was watching them both with an unreadable expression.

Interpreting that as the signal to get ready for bed, Seon grabbed his sak and got his blanket out. He went off to a corner by himself again and stretched out. Just as he was settling in, Alix landed in front of him and dropped a rabbit at his feet. Seon stared at it with disbelief. He looked up and saw that both Corin and Azoz had similar expressions.

"Wow," Azoz cried. "Why didn't we think of that!"

Seon grinned, picked up the rabbit between his thumb and forefinger, and tossed it to Azoz. Then he reached into his pouch and tossed Alix a berry, which she caught deftly in her beak.

"Good girl, Alix," he said softly. "You are the best."

Azoz just shook his head and went over to the fire to begin cleaning the rabbit. Seon could hear him talking quietly to Corin about drying the meat out. He smiled softly to himself. If he trained Alix to help him, hunting wouldn't be so bad after all.

A little while later, Azoz came back over to his blanket.

"Hey, Seon," he said softly. "Are you awake?"

"Yeah," Seon answered back. "How'd you do it?"

"Corin helped me use the fire."

"That's amazing."

"Energy is energy."

"It's still amazing."

"Yeah, it was." There was a pause. "It's also amazing that you got Alix to get a rabbit for you. How'd you do that?"

"Honestly? I don't know." Seon laughed softly. Some things could be so if wishing made them so, apparently.

"Do you think you can do it again?"

"Yeah. Yeah, I think I can. Hopefully I won't have to do it ... you know, the way you said."

"You really don't want to hunt, do you?" Azoz asked.

"I really don't," Seon told him, as emphatically as a person can in a near whisper.

"You're not going to eat it? The meat I mean?"

"Is he going to make me?" Seon asked.

"I don't know."

"You don't know?"

There was a pause. Seon found himself wondering about the question and his question and Azoz's answer. Deep down, he'd been worried since it first came up.

"Have you ever disobeyed him?"

There was silence. To Seon, that seemed like an answer in itself. He'd known the answer to that question before he even asked it. Azoz was cocky and irreverent, but Corin was unyielding and stern. Seon was just along for the ride on this journey. He was a participant. Azoz was Corin's apprentice and the one who had to be obedient.

"Seon?"

Azoz's voice came out of the dark, so quiet he could barely hear it.

"Yeah?"

"I think you had better eat the meat."

Chapter 8

As they continued the journey, the landscape began to change. Seon was not enjoying the continuous walking, even though he had to admit that the boots made it easier on his feet than he thought it otherwise would have been. They stopped far less than he would have wanted to. They talked far less than he was used to, but that didn't bother him. Relations with his traveling companions were frosty at best. The environment was far less ... normal than he was used to.

Everything was the same, yet not the same. The world around him looked as if it had been drawn and colored by a small child. None of the plants and animals were the way he was expecting them to be. The leaves on the trees were the wrong shape and size. The insects had either more wings or fewer legs. The colors were brighter and richer. Everything was either larger or smaller than he was used to.

Seon knelt next to a small clover that had eight tiny leaves. It was a bright pink color that looked like the hue of the medicine his mother used to give him for stomach aches when he was little, striped with veins of an even more vivid tone. He gave it an experimental sniff, almost expecting it to give off the sweet scent of bubble gum. He strongly suspected it was poisonous. Where he came from, brighter colors were a warning. Here, they seemed to be the norm.

All around him, there were shades of green as he was used to. But the spectrum did not end there. Every other color seemed to be represented in everything from the pebbles on the ground to the birds in the trees. Seon's own familiar stood out in the drabness of otherwise gorgeous plumage. Alix's copper-colored feathers did not blend into trees with fuchsia-colored leaves. That didn't stop her from finding prey, however, as she was currently enjoying a prune-colored mouse-like creature.

Leaving Alix to the meal, Seon sat cross-legged on the soft bed of multicolored leaves and closed his eyes. He reached out with his senses, getting in tune with the environment around him. It was an exercise he liked to use to calm his nerves and get his bearings. This place was so different, so unlike his own world, that he felt the need to understand it.

He could hear the sound of the slight breeze rustling through the trees, with Alix crunching on the mouse-meal high about him. He felt that same breeze tickle his skin, brushing lightly over him like a breath. The air around him smelled faintly musty, a mixture of underbrush and tree bark, and he breathed in the scent as if it could satiate some need he hadn't realized was there.

With this new awareness, Seon could sense the thousands, maybe millions, of beings in the forest around him. He interacted with a few of them in passing, subtle glimpses into minds that made little sense to him. At first, he flitted from one small mind to another before finally settling in. It was an exercise that Corin had wanted him to practice. As disorienting as it was to try to understand the world from a tiny insect's viewpoint, after some time, Seon began to appreciate how it saw the world and took over to direct one, and then many, of the microscopic winged creatures.

"Looks like you're getting the hang of it," Seon heard Azoz comment drily.

He opened his eyes to view his handiwork. Hovering a few feet in the air in front of him was a small pebble of a violently blue color. At any other time before, Seon would have thought it was magic if he'd seen something like this. He knew better now.

Shrugging, Seon let off his concentration and the pebble dropped to the forest floor. Azoz eyed it sardonically, as if expecting it to now walk off on its own. He walked over and nudged it with his boot.

"Not bad," he said.

Seon shrugged. He didn't need recognition from Azoz of all people. So, in response, he narrowed his eyes and said nothing.

"Like magic?" Azoz said.

Ignoring his smirk, Seon looked up at the trees and whistled, bringing Alix down to land on his shoulder. He started to walk away.

"How'd you do it?" Azoz called after him.

Not bothering to answer, Seon walked through the forest back toward their camp. He had already determined that Azoz's arrival meant that it was time for him to return. Corin didn't seem to mind him leaving and wandering off on his own for a certain amount of time but there were limits to his freedom. Seon was not going to accept his role as captive willingly. He walked ahead of Azoz, ignoring the other's attempts at conversation.

Azoz, for his part, treated Seon like the whole thing was a lark most of the time. He was rarely serious and Seon tired of the jibes and cocky grins sent in his direction. This was not as fun for Seon as it apparently was for him.

"No, really, how did you?" Azoz said again, still as cheerfully.

Seon continued to ignore him. Azoz could pretend they were buddies all he wanted. Seon didn't have to humor his captors.

Since outwardly antagonizing Azoz never seemed to work, Seon had decided to ignore him. He knew that picking a fight with the taller boy would end in disaster. Azoz had more muscle and training than Seon could ever dream of, and he would love nothing more than to tussle with Seon. For his part, Seon knew it would come to that sooner or later. He would rather fight Azoz than Corin, against whom he had no chance at all. He glanced at Azoz. He had no chance there either.

"I was just practicing communing with nature, like I was told to," Seon said.

He made no effort to keep the bitterness out of his voice. If he was honest with himself, he enjoyed his forays into the forest. It was peaceful and the plants and animals were different enough here that there was always something new to see. It also got him away from Azoz's jovial chatter and Corin's severe gaze. Yet he was frustrated with being told what to do, where to go, or how long he could be there. His old life had been blissfully dull, and his new existence seemed fraught with tension by comparison.

"'Communing with nature,'" Azoz repeated mirthfully. "That's funny."

The boy seemed to get genuine glee out of the phrase and that just annoyed Seon more. Even sarcasm tickled Azoz. Seon hadn't meant to be funny. He knew that walking the fine line between irreverence and insolence was risky with Corin, but Azoz seemed to live on that line. Corin was so stern and ill-tempered that Seon couldn't imagine that he had a sense of humor. The two were a strange combination and Seon had no idea how they'd ever ended up paired together.

Fortunately, Azoz seemed to give up on pestering Seon on the way back to camp. He pleasantly but silently walked beside Seon the rest of the way as if they were just two friends taking a stroll. Seon risked a sideways glance and saw that Azoz wasn't even looking at him. His eyes were on the trail ahead. Finally able to relax, Seon concentrated more on the woods around them as they walked.

It was almost midday. This meant there was bound to be a confrontation when Seon arrived at the camp. He wondered if Azoz enjoyed that kind of thing. Maybe he was so used to quarreling with Corin himself that he was just happy to see someone else as the object of the man's ire. Seon wasn't looking forward to it. He wasn't afraid of Corin, but he wasn't prepared to see how far the man would go if Seon continued to push him.

"Don't look so cheerful," Seon muttered when they were almost to the camp.

"What are you about?" Azoz knew exactly what Seon meant. His eyes were practically gleaming in anticipation.

Seon grunted. "You go," he said. "I'm not going."

"Scared?" Azoz scoffed. "Where will you go, then?"

"I don't know. Back home."

As soon as he said it, Seon knew it was ridiculous. They had kidnapped him and taken him to someplace that might as well be another planet for all he recognized it. Not even the plants and animals were of the same species. Of course, they wouldn't be. If you traveled to a new continent, things would be different. This was something else though. Something so much more than a difference of ecology. The plants and animals here were tapped into an energy that he had never seen before, at least not at these levels.

By now, Azoz realized Seon saw the futility of bluffing. For once, he wasn't smirking or sending Seon his signature cockeyed grin. Instead, he seemed more serious than usual.

"How many times is it now?" he asked.

"Three."

"What did he say last time?"

"Not to come back without meat."

Azoz nodded thoughtfully. Seon looked down at his feet

because he couldn't think of what else to do. Suddenly the world around them seemed quiet and still in a way that wasn't really possible.

"What about Alix?" Azoz asked hopefully, seeing the hawk come flitting down on Seon's shoulder. "She's done it before."

"She has," Seon responded slowly.

"What difference does it make where it comes from as long as you bring it?"

"And what do you care?" Seon demanded.

Azoz looked hurt. Seon was surprised to see a genuine emotion on his face, but there it was. He might have actually cared about Seon in some weird way, as if they were together on an adventure. It made Seon feel sad for him.

"Don't worry, it's not what you think," Azoz finally answered, with more bitterness than Seon expected. "He'll just take it out on me."

Seon figured that was probably true, though it was more honesty than he expected from Azoz. He reached up and gently stroked the mottled brown feathers on Alix's chest. It was a tough call, deciding between an act of clear rebellion and avoiding inevitable conflict.

"Seon," Azoz said, his voice low and full of emotion, "just do it."

Finding himself frustrated by his own desire to give in, Seon sighed. He concentrated on the image of a rabbit and reached out with his senses. Just a small way off, there was one foraging in a clearing. He sent the image and location to Alix, who took off straight for it. Within minutes, she was back with the creature.

"Nice," Azoz smirked.

As much as Seon wanted to smack the smirk off his face, he ignored him. Instead he praised Alix and gave her a piece of dried meat, then sighed and stuffed the dead rabbit into his sak. He cooed and petted her for a few moments and then walked a few more feet before sending her off again, this time for something that looked like a large, fat, badger that was mustard-colored with red stripes. He settled for carrying that by its feet, disgusted with himself the entire way.

When they came into camp, Seon dumped the larger animal down next to the campfire and then opened his sak and tossed the smaller one down next to it. Without a word, Azoz plopped down next to them and began skinning the rabbit. Corin said nothing to either of them. Seon was almost disappointed. His nerves were on edge, and the lack of a fight was nearly a letdown. He wasn't foolish enough to pick one though.

As usual, Seon refused to eat the meat with the others. He sat and ate his berries and fiercely returned Corin's glare. It was not a hunger strike. It was principle. They couldn't feel the animal from the inside the way he could.

Azoz ignored them. He had already told Seon he thought he was being stubborn on purpose. Seon hadn't bothered to explain. He didn't owe them an explanation. They were not going to try to understand—at least Corin wasn't. In Seon's opinion, Corin's insistence that Seon use his affinity for animals to hunt was cruel at best. This exploitation of his abilities was unfair. While it was true that the party had to eat, Seon didn't see why he had to be the one to supply them. He was perfectly willing to gather berries, tubers, morels, and anything else that didn't have a conscious thought.

As soon as the tense meal was eaten, Azoz went off to prepare the furs and Seon wandered to the edge of the camp as he'd grown accustomed. He sat cross-legged on the dirt and focused on clearing his mind. That step accomplished, he reached out with his consciousness for impressions of beings around him. There were many, of course, from the tiny insects in the air above and crawling on the log nearby to the small animals scurrying in the brush. Farther away, larger beasts hunted in the forest. Seon chose one of these, concentrating on it until he could see what it could see, smell what it could see, and feel what it could feel.

It was a disorientating experience. The animal was a large omnivore, about the size of a bear. It was currently scrounging through the forest for berries, but Seon sensed its hunger for something more substantial. It was not averse to a small animal or something bigger. He felt and experienced it lift its head and sniff the air, then rear up on its hind legs. There was something there, not far off. The beast lumbered through the forest at a speed slower than Seon would have expected. Seon was just along for the ride today though. He wasn't here to influence, only to experience. He didn't interfere as his host came upon another of its kind in a clearing in the woods, mauling a deer-like prey.

Now that he could see the smaller one, he knew what the one he was inhabiting looked like. The bear-like creatures were emerald-green in color and had large paws with sharp, vicious-looking claws on the ends. They were the shape and size of bears, but their heads were more like a big cat's, such as a cougar—round with pointed ears that had tufts of hairs coming out. Seon could see long, pointed teeth.

There was a power-play of sorts between the two bear-creatures, as Seon's reared up on its hind legs and made a roaring sound, pawing through the air. Seon heard the sound and watched through eyes that seemed like his. His bear-cat must have been bigger, even though he couldn't really tell from his vantage point, because the other one ran off. With a noise of triumph, what was left of the carcass disappeared. Seon didn't taste it, but he could sense the beast's satisfaction and watch it as it ate.

Not enjoying the spectacle, Seon withdrew from the animal's consciousness. The experience made him wonder if he could have changed the bear's mind and caused it to run away instead of stealing the meal from his rival. There was no reason to do so, other than to see if he could. He had been able to affect the crows' behavior, and the insects that had worked together in lifting the pebble. Hundreds of tiny insects could lift a small pebble, making it look as if it were hovering in mid-air. The more he worked on his control and practiced the exercise, the more Seon thought of ways he could use this Gift.

It also made him wonder if it would work as well at home. He had done things like this before, influencing the cab driver and healing Alix. He had worked with plants to make them grow faster and healthier and heal them when they were sick or dying. This place had a different energy. Connecting was easier in a way he couldn't explain. True, he had more training now. Corin had explained the process to him and had him practice it, and he had used it more. The difference was there though, in a way he couldn't quite put his finger on. It was as if he had to reach out and grasp it in both places, but he had to reach farther at home. Here, it was so much easier. He did not have to reach as far because everything seemed to depend on a level of energy use that wasn't found back home.

When Azoz insisted there was no such thing as magic, this was what he meant. Everything revolved around energy and every living thing used that energy in some way. The magic-wielders, as they were known, were just able to harness it in a way that others could not or would not do.

Seon stood up and returned to the camp, stretching and then walking slowing. The process of returning to himself could be disorienting, especially when he had inhabited the consciousness of such a raw creature as the bear-cat. He was glad in a way that the bear-cat had found another of its kind, so he could see what it had looked like. Most of the time on these excursions, he never knew.

As soon as Seon returned to the camp, he sat down on his bedroll. Despite his affinity for animals, he was grateful for the soft fur lined with cloth. He knew there was some kind of special spell woven into the lining. He could feel that it was softer and warmer than it would otherwise be. Everything in his kit was enhanced in some way. Even though he had been forced on this journey against his own will, Seon had to admit that his gear was first-rate.

Never one to worry where he wasn't wanted, Azoz sidled over to where Seon was sitting. Seon ignored him, busying himself with looking through his foraging sacks to sort through the berries, mushrooms, and other edible finds he had found that day. Azoz reached over and popped a sour berry into his mouth playfully. Seon resisted the urge to roll his eyes. He had learned the gesture meant nothing to Azoz.

"Can you please go over to your own side?" Seon groused.

"Why? It's just us here anyway," Azoz took out his knife and began to whittle at a piece of wood.

Seon didn't know why this hobby continued to annoy him. He should just ignore it. It seemed pointless, since all Azoz did was throw away the half-designed pieces. He could not help but look up in interest though at Azoz's last statement.

"Where did he go?"

Azoz shrugged and kept whittling. Apparently, he agreed with Seon that if Corin wasn't there they were better off, with no one to glower at them and give them orders. Seon thoughtfully chewed on a sweetleaf. They were one of his favorite finds from the area, like a twist between chewing gum and taffy.

Corin's tendency to disappear for days at a time was to his advantage, but it also made him curious. He wondered where the man went and what he was doing. Since there was no way he was going to ask and Azoz apparently wasn't going to either, it didn't seem like he was going to find out any time soon. Seon realized he hadn't even noticed Corin leave because he had been so caught up in his bear-cat experience.

"I guess I don't have to worry about hunting for a while."

"We will live on berries?" Azoz quipped.

"There's more than berries here," Seon pointed out.

He was proud of the haul he'd found in the last couple of days. There was more variety as he had become accustomed to the landscape and the plants and animals here. The wider color palate had thrown him off at first. Some of the fruits and legumes laid out on the bedroll in front of him he would have previously dismissed as poisonous if he'd seen them in the wild or thought they were artificially colored if he saw someone eating them at home. Now that he was used to the vibrant colors, he enjoyed the new flavors that came with them.

"I'm supposed to work with you on hand-to-hand," Azoz said.

There was no inflection to his voice either way, but Seon made a face. He didn't mind training with Azoz for the most part. He preferred it to Corin, whose clipped orders and scorching glares irritated him even though he didn't want to admit that sometimes the man made him nervous. Azoz also made him wary, but for different reasons. In moments of loneliness, he sometimes found himself wanting to make friends with the boy. They were the same age. They were in the same boat, in some ways. Seon was the prisoner, but Azoz was also subject to Corin's mercurial moods.

"I suppose now is as good a time as ever," Seon said.

He stood up, and Azoz popped up beside him. He often wondered where Azoz got all his energy from. He certainly seemed to possess an endless enthusiasm. Seon didn't have much time for another thought because Azoz was on him, attacking immediately. He had a hands-on approach to teaching which seemed to consist of beating the stuffing out of Seon and then asking him what he'd done wrong later.

This time was no different. Seon tried to block Azoz as the blows rained down. He was mostly unsuccessful, as usual. There were two or three shots he was able to return, but his mind was barely able to keep up a blow-by-blow summary. Frustrated by his inability to keep up, as usual, Seon found himself retreating into his mind in much the same way he did during his trances. Surprisingly, this allowed him to focus on Azoz as if he could sense his thoughts and where he would go next. The fight was over much more quickly, because Seon was finally able to block some of the shots. He still could not block all of them, because even when Seon knew what Azoz was about to do, the other boy was that much faster. Still, the fight did not end with Seon in a crumpled and bloody heap, which he took for a win.

"That was amazing," Azoz said after waiting a few minutes. "How did you do it?"

Seon didn't respond. He was still sore, bleeding, and disoriented from the experience. He wasn't quite sure what happened or how he had done it in the first place. It was yet another manifestation of his Gift, and he wasn't sure if Corin had known it would work that way or if it was just something that he had developed on his own.

"Well?" Azoz demanded. "Own up. We're going to have to tell him."

Since that was true enough, Seon looked down at his hands appraisingly, then closed his eyes, took a deep breath, and focused. When he opened his eyes, his hands were clear of the scrapes and there was no longer blood dripping from his nose. He looked up to see Azoz smirking at him and felt his face. The swelling he'd felt developing was gone now, and he realized he could see more clearly. Azoz must have given him a black eye too.

"Wicked," Azoz said.

Seon couldn't help feeling a bit smug at impressing him. It was the first time he had held his own in a fight, even if it was through his manipulation of Azoz's mind and not through his skill at fighting. It would take months and probably years to get to the point where he would have the strength and skill to hold his own in a fight, let alone win one. Having something that he could use in the meantime was a relief.

"It just kind of happened," Seon admitted. "I don't really have anything to tell him either. I don't even know if I can do it again."

"Well, we have to practice later," Azoz said.

For the first time, that idea did not fill Seon with dread. Azoz might not beat Seon to a pulp this time. If he could master this skill, he might even be able to hold his own in a fight against opponents who were actually trying to hurt and kill him. He knew Azoz had no such intentions. He only did as much damage as he did because he knew Seon could heal it almost instantly.

"You're on," Seon said with a grin.

Chapter 9

The sun was coming up the next morning when Seon slowly opened his eyes. He could feel the warmth on his face, and his other senses were also awash with input. The more he had become aware of his gifts, the more he had come to notice how he relied on other senses more. He had used his vision in different ways, but the other senses too. There was something disconcerting about lying there feeling the sun on his face but also smelling the air the way the small animals in the brush around him did or listening for predators like they did. This wasn't something he consciously chose to do anymore. He realized he was doing it only after he was fully awake.

Azoz kept insisting this wasn't magic, but no one back home had these skills. He had never seen anyone control lightning before, or manipulate a murder of crows, or heal people or animals. It didn't matter what it was called, gifts or magic. It was something special that not everyone can do. Based on what Azoz and Corin had told him, it also made some people afraid. It explained a lot about the search for Emili that Azoz repeatedly told him was not a rescue.

Lack of contact with Emili was also worrying Seon. Since he had been kidnapped, he had not heard from her. Corin and Azoz had asked him about this, and he wasn't sure they believed his denials. Azoz's reaction was typical of Azoz—he thought it was funny. Azoz could be as sardonic as he wanted, but Seon knew that Corin would only be patient for so long. They were counting on Seon to bring them to Emili, and he really had no idea where she was. They only knew the general direction to go in for so long, and then they would need specifics.

Seon also missed their communication, and the casual conversations they had without words. Emili was his friend in a way he'd never been close with anyone before. They understood each other. Seon realized that she too was kidnapping him in a way, by calling him relentlessly until he could do nothing but obey her summons, so strong was the urge to obey. After they had met, however, he had grown to enjoy her company more than people he saw in person every day. She struck him as tough, honest, and kind. He could tell all of this from their interactions but was somehow nervous about meeting her in person.

It was not that Seon expected Emili to be different from the version of her he had been spending time with in his dreams. He knew this was the genuine version of herself. He was more concerned about Azoz and Corin and their plans for her. They expected him to bring them to her. He had no choice but to do so. If he didn't, he would never see her. That wasn't his biggest concern. He could live with never meeting her. He couldn't live with the guilt of what might happen when they found her. In leading them to her, he might be betraying her instead of saving her.

It was these musings that Seon was pulled from by the realization that Azoz was standing over him. He opened his eyes slowly. Azoz grinned, handing him the usual stone mug of warmed porridge.

"Thanks," Seon said.

He was grateful for the food. The morning meal was one time he didn't have to argue over what they were eating, since it was just the mixture of grains and berries with no meat. Seon suspected there was reconstituted cream in the recipe because it tasted so good, but he had never minded eating products from animals that didn't involve killing the animal as long as the livestock was humanely kept. Given the lack of technological advancement in this society, he doubted factory farming was commonplace. Regardless, eggs and dairy were an area where Seon was willing to pick his battles for now. He had never been a vegan, even back home.

The two sat in companionable silence eating for the next few minutes. When they were finished, Seon cleaned the mugs with the special 'magic' dust the way Azoz had taught him. When they set off into the woods to forage, Alix returned from her own hunting to fly in wide circles overhead as they walked. There was little conversation as Seon concentrated on reaching out his senses for hungry small animals doing the same thing, following their trails to berries, nuts, and edible greens. Azoz also contributed, using his own skills in locating mushrooms growing in the shade of the forest canopy. In no time at all, the two had gathered several days' worth of food to replenish their dwindling stock, even without Seon eating the dried meat from last night. If Corin didn't return, they wouldn't need to look for food for some time.

They stopped by the creek bank to have a snack. Seon had removed his shoes and socks and both of them were hanging their feet in the creek while Alix hopped around taking a bath and catching small fish. Azoz seemed to be enjoying himself as much as Seon was.

"Want to practice sparring some more?" Azoz asked.

Seon shook his head. He wanted to laze around by the side of the creek as long as possible, even though he knew that wasn't likely to happen. Even so, he'd rather not spend his time getting beaten up.

"Why not," Azoz asked. "You're getting better."

Seon shrugged. He did need to practice his skills, but he was a little nervous about his use of his Gift in the process. While he realized he needed to, it was unnerving, and he didn't really want to get better at it if it meant learning to read the minds of people as well as animals. He had gotten used to working the skill with animals, but humans were another matter. It was just too much to think about.

"Come on," Azoz said. "On your feet."

Seon made a face but complied. He dropped his sack by the creek and didn't bother with his boots, since he noticed Azoz hadn't put his on either. The creek bank was a beach of soft sand with only a sprinkling of glittery pebbles that didn't hurt when they were stepped on. Facing off against Azoz, Seon swallowed and tried to hide his nervousness. Getting better at anticipating his opponent's moves through some weird kind of telepathy was not the same as being able to fight back properly when that same opponent was bigger, stronger, and faster.

Since Azoz was obviously waiting for Seon to make the first move, Seon backed up. He wasn't sure why he backed up, but he did. His first instinct was to run away. He didn't care if that made him a coward. If they were supposed to be practicing what he might do in a real-world fight, running seemed the best choice when he was outmatched by his opponent.

"Don't bother," Azoz said. His voice seemed to say that he was either bored or amused. It was probably both, knowing Azoz.

"How did you know what I was going to do?" Seon asked, purposely not saying what he had been going to do.

"Your feet," Azoz said, pointing down.

Seon looked down. Sure enough, his feet were pointed off to the right, in the direction he had been thinking of running. He found this both enlightening and frustrating. He was going to have to watch that. He might have his Gift to let him into people's thoughts, but Azoz had training and experience to do the same thing.

Trying not to let Azoz know how that little bit of information had gotten to him, Seon took two steps forward. He realized too late that this move probably played into Azoz's hands when Azoz chose that moment to strike. Despite the number of times they had sparred, with or without Corin watching, Seon was still surprised by how quickly and silently Azoz moved. He slammed into Seon with a concise uppercut to the jaw that sent him spiraling and made him instantly dizzy.

As Seon was knocked back, he tried to gather his thoughts and also break his way into Azoz's mind as he had before. He knew that Azoz was making no efforts to keep him out. He idly wondered why that was as he took another dizzy step to the side and tried to block Azoz's deft swing. He just needed an opening. Unfortunately, he wasn't getting one.

"Come on! You can do better than this!"

Seon wasn't sure whether that was taunting or encouragement. It wasn't having either effect because he barely heard it. Azoz's voice was dim, as if he was on the other end of a long tunnel. Seon was trying to concentrate on too many senses at once by focusing on his own break into Azoz's, and it wasn't working. As opposed to the first time when he had accidentally felt what Azoz was going to do and acted on instinct, this time he was acting with intention, and it was muddying him up. The end result was a frustrating jumble of sensations that Seon couldn't unravel fast enough to act on any one input.

Azoz's final blow made contact, and Seon went down. He almost felt that the knockout was a mercy move. Seon felt nothing but relief even as he fell to the sand in a heap. There he remained, groaning in defeat. He felt more confused than embarrassed or hurt, even though he was in plenty of physical pain.

As Seon's eyes were squinted closed, he felt rather than saw a shadow fall over him. He could tell that Azoz was holding down a hand to him in the universal offering of support and help up. Seon sighed and took the offered hand, even though he wanted nothing more to lay in the sand. Instead of allowing Azoz to pull him up, he yanked Azoz down into the sand next to him, where he fell with a thump. Rather than be annoyed, the boy just laughed.

"Fair enough," Azoz grunted, brushing sand from his tunic.

Seon shrugged. It wasn't compensation for losing the fight. He really just didn't want to get up yet. He was tired, frustrated, and a bit warm. The sun was rising into the sky, and he could feel its warmth overhead just a little too uncomfortably. The gentle rushing of the creek just yards away called refreshingly.

"I don't know if it's going to work," Seon admitted, more candidly than he usually was. "I don't know if it's because I am rubbish at fighting or because you're a person. Animals are simple. Of course, it might just be because you are so good at fighting."

"I appreciate the assessment," Azoz said wryly, "but I think it's a bit from each bucket. You just have to practice. You'll get the hang of it. I have an idea."

"What?" Seon asked, when after a moment Azoz did not speak.

"Why don't we start by keeping it simple. Try to get what I'm thinking without anything else. I won't move or talk, or try to hit you," Azoz said.

Seon thought that through. It seemed like a good idea, and also not. It could be a trap. Reading someone's mind, or whatever it was called, without anything else, seemed creepy and intrusive.

He did it all the time with Emili, but it was so different with her. It was an exchange of conversation, just like exchanging words. Somehow Seon never could imagine the same thing happening with Azoz.

"All right," Seon said slowly. "Think of an image. Sort of like a word, but in an image, that you want to say to me."

"Okay."

"Ready."

Azoz held a hand out, palm up. Seon recognized that as the signal to stop. That's what it meant at home, anyway. Then Azoz gestured his palm up. Seon figured that meant to continue. He closed his eyes and reached out as usual with his sense, trying to perceive where his consciousness ended and Azoz's began. He felt a human being right away, just as he would have seen him with his eyes open. Azoz was a bundle of senses the same way an animal would be, but his senses were different. Animals focused more strongly on certain senses and they experienced them differently, depending on the animal. Azoz experienced the world in a similar way to Seon's experience, which was why Seon had gotten so confused before.

Now that things were calmer and slower though, Seon could tell that Azoz was different. Seon wondered why that was. It could be that Azoz was a different species from Seon, and not just a different race or nationality as Seon had assumed. After all, no one where Seon came from had green hair or yellow skin. Perhaps the difference came from training. Azoz had been trained to use his senses and the energy from nature, just as Seon was learning to do. The gap was that he was much more advanced at the process. This was a revelation to Seon. This difference in perception was a revelation to Seon. He had assumed that the animals in this world had developed different senses, the way they did in his own. He had no idea that he could develop his Gift to use his senses to this degree. That he could perceive the world so differently was both exciting and terrifying to Seon. He would never be the same.

From Azoz's perspective, colors were richer and had hues that Seon had ever seen. There were simply more on the spectrum. In the shadows where Seon could only perceive movement in darkness, Azoz saw not only shapes but images almost as complete as if they were being seen in daylight. His ears perceived the smallest pebble shifted by a four-legged amphibian slithering out of the creek. Movement flickered, almost as if in slow motion. No wonder Azoz was so fast.

"Well?" Azoz asked.

"Oh," Seon had been so distracted he had forgotten to look for the image. "You must be hungry. You're showing me a stew cooking over a fire."

With a delighted laugh that was almost a cackle, Azoz's eyes popped open, and he sat up. "Indeed! What was in it? What did it smell like?"

Seon resisted the urge to roll his eyes. He really was going to have to let that gesture go. It was childish anyway. "Why did you have to get so specific, anyway? It had morels, those purple tubers, and the funny pink mushrooms you like so much that I hate. Also, onions. Are you happy?"

"Only if you cook it," Azoz said with a devious grin.

"Right," Seon shrugged. "You heat the water and clean up after then."

"Deal."

The two had a tranquil meal, and it was one of the first times that Seon could remember feeling relaxed during the trip. It might have been the fact that the two were not at odds over anything at the moment, or the fact that Azoz did not seem to expect Corin back for a few days. That made both of them more at ease. For all of Azoz's bluster, he clearly was not interested in antagonizing Corin. Seon understood that, but he didn't feel that he needed to answer to the man. That didn't mean he was stupid though. Seon didn't want to provoke Corin either, even though he wasn't Corin's apprentice.

After the meal was eaten, Azoz cleaned up. Seon ate his fill of the stew, because there was no way to save it. He normally wasn't a big eater, but Azoz seemed to eat as much as there was to eat, and Seon was learning to take his cue from that. It made sense that food wasn't always easy to come by when traveling by foot and mostly foraging and hunting for food, especially when Seon would not eat the meat.

The two headed off into the woods, back toward their camp. Alix rode on Seon's shoulder this time. The sun was high in the afternoon sky now, and the canopy of the trees overhead left a cool shade that felt refreshing. Seon tied his cooling handkerchief over his neck anyway but left his hat off. As long as they were in the woods, he would not need it. He kept his senses close, so as not to be overwhelmed by the sheer enormity of life in the forest.

"That was good," Azoz said. "You are not a bad trail cook. Of course, it would have been better with some of that *lapus* in it. I do not know why you refuse to eat the meat."

"I've already told you," Seon said. "Once I'm in its head, I don't want it in my body."

"That makes no sense," Azoz scoffed. "Food is food."

Seon made a face. He was tired of this argument. As far as he was concerned, they would never understand and there was sense in trying to make them. As long as Seon didn't starve and they didn't force him to eat the animal meat, everything would be fine.

"I don't want to, so what does it matter?" Seon said.

"What if we run out of berries?" Azoz asked.

"There is plenty to eat besides berries," Seon insisted.

"What about insects? You are in their heads too. Will you eat them? You care about their feelings?" Azoz replied.

Without even looking at Azoz walking behind him, Seon could see the smirk on his face. He didn't bother getting frustrated. Seon was pretty sure this conversation was just to pass the time for Azoz. It mattered not to him whether Seon ate meat. Corin could order Seon to hunt and he had to do it, or at least he had been doing it because he didn't want to find out what would happen if he didn't. Azoz had no place in the argument, as far as Seon was concerned.

"What do you care?" Seon finally asked. "More meat for you."

When Azoz didn't answer. Seon stopped. He looked back and realized Azoz hadn't answered because he had stopped walking. He was clearly listening. Seon hadn't been paying attention, and he had let his guard down during this ridiculous argument. Azoz clearly hadn't. He heard something. Alix must have as well, because she took flight.

Seon reached out with his senses. Something was coming— something big. He had no idea what it was, but he could tell it was hungry, it was vicious, and it knew they were there.

"Run, Azoz!" Seon cried.

Azoz shook his head. He pulled his knife out of the sheath in his boot. Knowing what he did of the animal coming for them, the knife looked wholly inadequate to Seon. He raced to Azoz and furiously grabbed him.

"No, Azoz. It's huge. We need to do something," Seon argued in desperation, trying to make Azoz understand.

Apparently Seon's tone got Azoz's attention. He must have

remembered in time that Seon had inside information—from inside the animal's senses. He looked around in quick appraisal.

"Go up a tree. Quick!"

Seon barely saw Azoz jump into the tree. He had no idea how he got there so fast. Seon's attention was currently on the animal charging at them. He saw it for a split-second before he entered its consciousness again. What came to mind was a cross between a rhinoceros and a cheetah, dark red with black spots and as large as a midsize car.

In the time he had, Seon didn't make any decisions. He just grasped at the largest impression he got from the animal and focused on that. The animal was *hungry*. That made sense to Seon. They were the biggest, loudest, and smelliest creatures in the forest at the moment. Seon grasped onto the animal's consciousness and tried to think of the strongest emotion he could. Hunger was a pretty strong instinct to overcome. He had to overcome hunger. Seon could only think of one thing.

Since he had no idea how to do it, Seon reached into his knife sheath with one hand, dividing his consciousness slightly. It was a risk he had to take. It was a move Corin had made him practice so many times he could do it in his sleep. Corin said this developed muscle memory. He would have to thank the man later because he was right. It took little conscious thought to get the knife. The next move also took no thought, because had he thought about it, he might not have been able to do it. Seon reached out and stabbed the knife into the fleshy part of his own thigh.

He did feel that pain. Then he grasped onto the sensation with all his might and threw it at the big cat. It worked. The cat was overwhelmed. Somewhere in the back of his mind, Seon heard a roar of pain in the distance.

The pain must have confused the creature. Since it felt pain but was not hurt, it must have decided Seon was the source of the pain. It turned tail and ran. Seon collapsed in a bleeding heap. He could hear Alix shriek.

Partly from exertion and partly from the wound, Seon found himself fighting loss of consciousness as he lost blood. He could hear Azoz talking to him. Apparently, he had dropped from the tree.

"Seon ... yourself? Seon? Are you there? Seon ... now!"

He could feel someone shaking him. There was also something in his mouth. Suddenly, he awaked with a jolt. Seon looked at Azoz with one bleary eye. The other one wouldn't open.

"Seon?"

"Ugh."

"I put a poultice on it. That was one crazy stunt you pulled," Azoz said. For once, his tone was completely serious.

"Oh."

"Why did you do that?" Azoz said, his voice sounding far away.

"I had to," Seon told him irritably. "I needed to make it feel pain."

"For Lovel's sake, couldn't you make it up?" Azoz cried.

"Uh," Seon grunted, trying to sit up as Azoz propped him up. "I don't know how to do that. I did the first thing I could think of so he wouldn't eat you."

"Okay, thanks," Azoz said. "You are telling Corin about this, not me."

Seon reached up and felt the side of his head. He still felt dizzy, and it also felt like he might have hit his head on a tree branch or a rock when he fell. Looking down, he saw a puddle of his own blood, which just made him want to sick up.

"I'm guessing you are too weak to heal yourself," Azoz said. "So, we are going to have to let the poultice and the healing root do it for a while."

"Healing root?" Seon asked.

"Yeah," Azoz nodded and held out a small mauve-green striped root for his inspection. "I think this will be part of your training. I know the basics. Everyone does. I can't do what you do, of course. That's a Gift. These are grown by Healers with the Gift."

That made sense. Seon had to admit it would be interesting to learn how to infuse plants with extra healing abilities than those they naturally had, and to work with the sick and injured. Since not everyone had the gift, it was something he seemed destined to do. Even though he did not trust Corin, he had to owe it to the man for finding him and showing him his potential, he supposed.

This line of thought always frustrated Seon. He hadn't been happy or feeling a sense of direction back home. Now he had one, should he choose to follow it. It was being forced that did not sit well with him. Of course, all he was really being forced to do was lead them to Emili. They had told him that he could return home after that. Leading them to Emili was bad enough though. Emili may not want to be found.

Seon looked up at Azoz and realized that he was being watched. He gave the boy a small smile. Alix was giving Sean an imploring look.

"I'll be alright," Seon said softly. "Let's just rest here for a while until I have the strength to walk. I am obviously not going to be good for much for a while. I think I am going to pass out in a minute here. Just watch me I guess, and make sure I wake back up. And keep an eye out for predators. You are obviously good at that."

Azoz nodded. "Of course, he said. "You rest. I will watch your back."

Chapter 10

After a few hours, Seon was feeling much better. He was leaned up against the tree, where his bedroll was making a comfortable pillow. Alix was perched on a branch above his head, keeping a wary eye out while Azoz kept him from being bored by telling stories of his childhood, which Seon found interesting because he still knew very little about Azoz or this world. Most of them were humorous, and Seon imagined that was by design. If Seon was laughing a little, he wasn't thinking about the pain he was in.

"How did you meet up with Corin?" Seon finally asked.

It was a question he had been wondering for a while. He knew obviously that Azoz was apprenticed to Corin, but not why or for how long. He was not sure who had chosen whom and he was sure it was an interesting story.

"Oh," Azoz looked thoughtful, as if he wasn't sure whether to tell the story or not. "Yeah, I guess that's a good story."

"Is it?" Seon asked hopefully.

Azoz gave a little laugh, "Well, I suppose it is. I was at *fundacional*, foundational, what you would call secondary school. A few years ago. In our culture, every child has to be apprenticed by the age of adulthood, but normally around twelve years old. I was nearly thirteen and no one had ever chosen me because I was incorrigible."

"Incorrigible?" Seon repeated with a grin.

"Well, yes," Azoz looked both sheepish and proud. "None of the teachers liked me much. I liked to work outside the rules a bit. Still do."

"Yes," Seon said with a snort. "I've noticed. So, what happened?"

"Well," Azoz said slowly. "One of my biggest problems was fighting with other kids. I have a temper, and other kids seemed to like to set me off to prove that they could win against me. Most of them couldn't, but they liked to try. I usually flattened them. It was particularly bad whenever any new kids came to our school. They wanted to prove they were tougher than me, and I was not going to back down. They fought me and I won."

Seon could only nod. He could see where this was going. Azoz looked neither proud nor remorseful. He was just stating facts.

"The teachers tried to stop me from fighting. They threatened me and punished me. It did not do any good. I was always in trouble for one thing or another anyway. I liked to play tricks on the teachers, other students, and visitors. It was so boring there that I had to do something to amuse myself. Most of the kids thought the pranks were funny. That is, unless they were the butt of my jokes. Then sometimes they did not find it as funny," Azoz shrugged.

"I can see that," Seon said bluntly. "It's bullying."

"I didn't mean it that way," Azoz said. "It was all in good fun."

"That's what they always say," Seon said.

Azoz ran a hand through his spiky green hair. "Well, as it was, a prank ended badly. I had meant to spike a rival's food with a potion I got from another student. I did not make it myself though. It is not my area of expertise. It was supposed to make his hair grow longer for a day. Like a girl. Instead, it fell out. All of it."

Seon gawked. He could see that scaring someone and angering him. Either version of the prank would be frightening, as a matter of fact.

"Wow," was all Seon could think to say.

"Yes," Azoz agreed. "So, he determined the source of the prank and challenged me. Naturally I did not back down. It was a legitimate challenge. We were interrupted by staff almost before we began though. The director tried to grab me, and I ran. I was not interested in the punishment for fighting."

"Where did you run to?"

Seon was getting interested in this story. He could picture it, even with the details Azoz was leaving out. The story was helping him understand Azoz boy more.

"I just ran. There was a meditation garden on the outskirts of the school grounds, and I ended up there. I just ran and was not even paying attention to where I was going. I was running along the stone path when I ran into Corin. I just ran into him," Azoz stopped to look at Seon self-consciously.

"Ha!" Seon said.

"Right," Azoz agreed. "I knew who he was, of course. He came by the school and temple often enough. I had never really interacted with him though. He had a reputation amongst the apprentice candidates, even though he hadn't had an apprentice in years."

Although Azoz did not say what Corin had a reputation for, Seon could guess. He had not spent much time with the man, but in that amount of time his impression was that he was unyielding and harsh. Azoz seemed to be managing just fine, but Seon suspected a large part of the reason was his skill and aptitude and his personality. Azoz was nearly unflappable and would always rather joke than take something seriously.

"He did not seem surprised to see me," Azoz went on. "He just held out a hand to stop me from bowling him over. Then he asked me what I was doing there. I told him I was running away because I had decided to leave school since no one would take me on as an apprentice. He asked me how old I was. When I told him, he said I still had time to find a mentor. I said there was no way any mentor would ever choose me, so I might as well leave."

"Corin ignored that altogether and asked me what had happened. He could tell I had been in a fight. I did not want to tell him, because then he would just scold me and take me back. So, I told him it was none of his business," Azoz said with a smirk.

"You did what?" Seon could not help but admire Azoz's nerve.

"Right. He said it was, because he was now my mentor," Azoz said. "I said there was no reason to take me on out of pity."

"What is the matter with you anyway?" Seon asked, shaking his head.

"I did not think that was the reason," Azoz explained. "I thought it was a trick, to get me back to school. He would take me to the director and then that would be the end of his interest in me."

"Oh," Seon said. "I guess I could see someone doing that. Corin doesn't seem the type though. He's strict and exacting, but not manipulative."

"Exactly," Azoz said. "Not in that way anyway."

Leaving Seon to wonder what that meant, Azoz laughed a small mirthless laugh. "I really do not know why, but I did tell him what happened. It just came pouring out. I had never felt like telling any of the teachers or staff. I guess maybe they never asked me, or never asked me the right way. Somehow, Corin asked the right questions to make me trust him and I ended up telling him everything. I never really felt like I belonged. My parents had sent me there when I was four, and ever since ..."

"Wait four? Why?" Seon asked.

"That is when they found out," Azoz said.

"Found out what?" Seon was still confused, but he was starting to get an idea.

"I was playing in the yard with my cat. I still remember that her name was Luc. I threw a ball for her, and she brought it back to me. We did this several times, usually until she got bored. Then she ran off. One day, I moved the ball by itself, and started playing as if Luc was still there. My mother saw me and said nothing. However, it was not long after that before some men came to take me away."

"Just for making a ball move on its own?" Seon said in disbelief.

"You have to understand," Azoz said, "people fear difference. The Umbra were in power then. They still are in many places. They do not tolerate the Gifted. Families who have children displaying Gifts usually run away in the night or ... the children disappear."

"Like you did," Seon said in a low voice.

"I am sure it was no mystery why," Azoz said. "No one would have spoken of it. In the village, people would have pretended my parents had no youngest son. My siblings will never speak my name again either."

"That's ridiculous," Seon said. "It's cruel."

"Is it better to be beaten for using your Gifts, in hope that you will stop using them or they will go away?" Azoz asked. "They do not go away, Seon. They are a part of us. They are who we are."

"I know that," Seon answered tensely.

"Well, then, I am better off than some." Azoz said. "At least my parents sent me away. They did not leave me in the woods."

Not wanting to think of parents who would do that to their own child, Seon stood up and stretched. He was relieved to feel only a slight amount of dizziness. Although he was nowhere near ready to heal himself, he felt comfortable standing and walking slowly around.

"Mine think I'm on a school field trip," Seon scoffed. "I sent them a two second plain text message. They didn't ask many questions now, did they?"

"Not everyone belongs in their family," Azoz said with the open-armed gesture that Seon was realizing was his equivalent of a shrug. "You are different. The first Gifted among your kind in a thousand years. You are bound to not quite fit in."

"Right," Seon said sardonically.

Azoz shook his head. "It is different for us. There are those that have Gifts and those who do not. It is not always safe to be in the middle."

"Who is in the middle?" Seon asked.

It seemed like Azoz either did not hear the question or wasn't going to answer it. Instead, he continued his story as if he had never left off. "Corin took me back to the *fundacional* and explained to them that he was going to take me on as an apprentice. I expected them to argue against it, but I think they were just glad to be rid of me."

"Do you leave, after that?" Seon asked. "School, I mean."

Azoz shook his head. "No. When a mentor takes on a new apprentice, he stays at the *fundacional* as an instructor. My education there was not complete. At first, you take classes with the other students and train independently with your mentor. Little by little, it is more time with your mentor and less time in classes. Eventually, there will be no classes."

"So, you are not there any more? At the ... the school?" Seon said.

"I still go there," Azoz said. "The staff and teachers do not mind me there as much. If I get in trouble now, they just have Corin deal with me."

"Right," Seon said, mostly to himself.

Somehow, he had the idea that Azoz still got into plenty of trouble. He wondered about this school, the *fundacional*. He was nervous that if he stayed, he would be sent there. Seon did not even speak the same language as Azoz. Every once in a while they talked in muted tones off to the side when Seon was not nearby. Azoz used words from the language occasionally but had never attempted to teach it to Seon.

"It will be fun, when you are there with me," Azoz said, looking at Seon.

"Me?" Seon asked.

"Of course," Azoz said with certainty. "You will have to attend classes and then train with a mentor."

"I really don't see how," Seon said. "I am not from here."

"You may not be," Azoz said. "But you are one of us just the same."

As he was mulling over those words, Seon considered what it would be like to be training with other kids who were like Azoz, and like himself. On the one hand the thought was intimidating. There was something encouraging about it though. He had always been the odd one out. Now he had something in common with the others, even though he still came from somewhere else. Maybe they were more the same than they were different.

"I don't even speak the language," Seon protested.

"Easy enough to learn," Azoz said.

"I have never really learned another language," Seon admitted. "It's not that common in my world."

"There are many dialects here," Seon said. "Everyone speaks the common language, and then the home dialect. I myself do not use that one much anymore. Not since ... I just do not need to."

Seon nodded. The reason why didn't need to be voiced out loud. He could tell that Azoz had not been back home to his village since he was a small child. Seon wasn't sure how he felt about that revelation. In some ways, he was relieved. He wasn't sure he would ever want to go back if it were him. He might not be going back either.

"Where do you think Emili is?" Seon asked, changing the subject.

"Why do you ask?" Azoz said.

"Will we be able to talk to her?" Seon wondered.

"Nothing seems to stop you now," Azoz pointed out.

"We don't use words," Seon told him.

"Oh," Azoz said. "Right."

This conversation reminded Seon that he hadn't communicated with Emili in some time. He wished he had a way to reach out to her, instead of always waiting for her to come to him. As it was, Seon was beginning to wonder if something had happened to her. Neither Azoz nor Corin had explained why it was so important to find her, but he had to assume the urgency meant she was in some kind of danger. Otherwise, it would not be so important to find her.

"Have you tried to reach her?" Azoz pressed. "Yourself, I mean."

"Of course, I have," Seon insisted.

He had. Many a night he had been flat on his back with his eyes pressed closed, waiting for her touch on his mind. When it didn't come, he had reached out to her, to no avail. He just wasn't sure how to reach her mind. If he knew how, he would have done it.

"Do you know where we're going?" Seon asked. "If you knew, you wouldn't need me, right?"

"We know up to a point," Azoz admitted. "As you know, we only know the general direction. "We have gone almost as far as we can on our own, I think. Soon, you will have to begin guiding us."

This filled Seon with a sense of dread. He had been thinking it was like this by the mood Corin had been in lately, which had been even worse than his usual dour demeanor. He expected Seon to have information he didn't have and had no way to get.

"What am I supposed to do, then?" Seon demanded. "I can't give you what I don't have. It's not my fault that you basically kidnapped me and forced me to come here when you knew I have no clue where she is."

"We didn't bring you because you know where she is," Azoz reminded him. "We brought you because you have a way of contacting her."

"But I don't!" Seon insisted. "You know I don't."

"I know no such thing," Azoz retorted. "You could contact her if you wanted to. You will find a way."

Seon walked a few steps away, blowing out a breath in frustration. He wasn't sure how to make Azoz understand. He wasn't being intentionally difficult. He had only found out he had special powers, or Gifts, or whatever they wanted to call them, a week before. They were expecting too much from him. They were training him in how to fight and how to use his powers to find food, heal, and communicate with animals and people across short distances. No one was teaching him how to communicate with a girl he barely knew across a great distance. There were so many things he was supposed to just figure out for himself.

"Find a way," Seon mumbled. "Right."

"Don't you want to?" Azoz asked in a voice that was more earnest than Seon was used to hearing from him.

"Sure, I do," Seon mumbled. "Fine. You make it sound so easy."

"It is," Azoz said. "You can reach into my thoughts. You can see into the animals when they are not anywhere close by. How is this any different?"

Shaking his head slowly, Seon paused on that question. He asked himself how it *was* different. It might be because Seon had always let Emili contact him first, or because she always had. Maybe he just expected her to. On the other hand, somewhere deep down maybe Seon just thought Emili was stronger than he was. She clearly knew what to do when he did not. She made him understand her. She had found him when no one else had. Seon had no idea how or why.

"It just is," Seon finally answered. "It is different."

At this response, Azoz made a 'suit yourself' gesture and walked to the edge of the clearing. It was late afternoon going into evening. The sun was high in the sky, but they were still cool under the forest canopy. They were comfortable and Seon had no desire to move, but he knew that they needed to leave before it got dark and head back to their camp.

"Let's go," he said. "I'm okay."

Without a word the two headed off. There was no conversation this time and they both were on high alert. Azoz was clearly watching the woods and listening, and Seon kept out of Azoz's head but reached out for animals in a wide circle around them, skipping from creature to creature as soon as he gauged that it was no threat. Eventually, they made their way back to camp in this manner. By that time, they were both exhausted from the day's events.

Seon reached into one of his saks and produced a mixture of nuts and berries. He tossed a handful onto a dried leaf and handed it over to Azoz, who accepted it wordlessly. Seon served himself a similar meal. That and water from their skins would have to serve them.

After he had eaten, Seon prepared his bedroll and stretched out on it. He closed his eyes and conducted his nightly meditation, though it was much earlier than usual. Trying to remember health instruction he'd had on concussions, he considered the possibility of sleep.

"Seon," Azoz said quietly.

"Yes?"

"I know you can do it."

"Really?" Seon knew the sarcasm was obvious regardless of the cultural difference. "How's that?"

"There is nothing so far you have not been able to do."

"Tell me a story, then."

"Very well," Azoz said. He reached into his medallion and removed the amethyst, something he almost never did. Perhaps he was looking for strength. "There's a story we tell to younglings—children. It's about a warrior named Jaysen. He gets visions, sort of like you. I guess that's what made me think of him. Anyway, he decides he needs to follow these visions, and they lead him into battle. He doesn't go alone though. He has a mentor, named Goram, and a sidekick, or a friend I guess, whose name changes in different stories. Sometimes it's an animal and sometimes it's a fellow traveler. In some stories his name is Kaydyn. There's more people with him in some versions. Of course he meets obstacles along the way. Kills people, rescues princesses, that sort of thing. In the end, he saves the Kingdom."

"What kingdom?" Seon asked.

"The kingdom doesn't have a name. It's just, 'the Kingdom'" Azoz said.

"Oh," Seon said. "I guess most cultures have stories like that."

"Maybe," Azoz said.

In the quiet that followed, Seon considered that statement. In a way, it was true. While he was still pretty terrible at fighting and pretty much refused to learn to hunt, he had learned most of what they were teaching him. In most cases, Corin or Azoz just told him what to do and had him practice it. There was no cause for the self-doubt.

Seon closed his eyes and measured his breathing. He focused on the picture in his mind of the field where he most often met with Emili. It was often the first image that came into focus when she called to him, and then she was there, and he was there with her. Seon decided to reverse the process. He imagined the field, and then pictured himself in it. Then he imagined Emili next to him.

At first, all he saw was the field of waving violet-colored grains as he always saw it. It was daylight there. The sun was low in the sky. Seon wondered if that meant they were in different time zones. The sky was a bright blue with gorgeous, slow-moving clouds. Seon could smell the musty-sweet smell of the slightly waving grains. There was a motion behind him. He turned quickly, but it was only a small rodent. When Seon turned around, he half-expected to see Emili there facing him, her dark hair in tresses woven around her head behind her ears and her light eyes dancing in joy to see him, so he could finally . There was nothing though. Nothing but the outline of the farmhouse way off at the edge of the fields and rolling amber hills on the horizon. Everything was somewhat hazy in the distance.

It did not work—at least not exactly. Seon was only able to

get the impression of the field. He was able to see the field. He was in the field. Something was wrong though. Seon did not understand what it was at first. Then suddenly he understood what it was. He needed to reach out with other senses than his eyes. He closed them and focused on his emotions.

Emili was communicating with him. She was close. He could not see her. He could feel that she was trying to tell him something. She was nearby, but she wasn't there in the field next to him. She was nowhere. She couldn't come to the field. Something was wrong. Seon couldn't sense what it was though. She was scared, or sad or nervous. He had no idea what it was she was trying to tell him. All he knew was that something was wrong.

Seon still had no idea where Emili was, or how to get to her. All he knew was that something wasn't right, even if he could not tell if she was in trouble or not. Emili needed help, and Seon had no idea how to help her. He desperately reached out to her, trying to tell her with his own emotions that he understood, that he was coming, and he would help her. The response was so immediate that he felt it like a physical force.

Emili was telling him in no uncertain terms not to come. She was in no danger now, but if he came for her, she certainly would be. Seon had no idea how he knew this. He also had no idea what to do about it.

Seon's eyes popped open. Back in their camp, the sun was setting. He could see Azoz over on the other edge of the camp, quietly whittling. For a moment, he considered telling him what he had seen and felt. After all, he had started to feel closer to Azoz in the last couple of days, especially after what they had been through today. Azoz had probably saved his life, and he had likely saved Azoz's first.

Then Seon remembered that he was still a prisoner. He had been taken against his will. He did not want that for her. He was not sure what they wanted from Emili. She might have more information than he did. He would wait, to see if she could contact him herself and tell him more. He would try again to contact her. He had to trust her. One thing was for certain. He did not trust Corin and Azoz yet.

Seon lay back down on his bedroll and began the slow, methodical process of healing his injuries from the day. He was still exhausted, but he was gaining more confidence in himself every time he went through the ritual. It was something he understood and accepted. As long as circumstances remained as they were, he would have to keep his wits about him and only trust himself.

Chapter 11

Seon grunted when Azoz nudged him with the toe of a boot and then he got up and fixed breakfast. Corin was nowhere to be seen, but that was hardly unusual. He was seen less and less, and that was more the better, as far as Seon was concerned. Lessons with Corin were grim and grueling. At least Azoz seemed to be interested in working with him and had some fun with him.

"I've been thinking," Seon said after they had finished cleaning up. "I want to change my name too."

"Really?" Azoz said, tossing his pack on. "Why? What made you think of that?"

With a shrug, Seon collected his gear and put his pack on his back and then picked up his foraging sack. He hadn't thought of it, actually. He wasn't even sure what had made him say it. Maybe it was a subconscious thought that had come out.

"I'm in another world. Maybe I should be another me," he said.

"That's ridiculous," Azoz said bluntly.

"No it's not," Seon said. "You had another name in my world. Why? People come from different countries to mine. It was an international school. And people make up names all the time. What makes your name so weird?"

"Have you heard it before?" Azoz demanded.

"Well, no," Seon answered honestly. "But so what?"

"Because names have power, that's what," Azoz said.

"Power?"

"Yes."

"What does that even mean?" Sean asked. "Besides, Corin used his own name."

"Corin used his name with me, and with you," Azoz said. "There was no danger with me, because I already knew it. With you, the danger was minimal because you were coming with us anyway."

"You didn't know that," Seon said.

Azoz just gave him a look. Seon didn't need to translate the look. Obviously they were sure enough that he was coming. If he hadn't agreed, they planned to just make him come. What had actually happened was somewhere in the middle. It made Seon frustrated to think about it, so he let the matter drop.

"Fine," he said. "Names have power. Why?"

"Why?" Azoz said. "Of all the ridiculous questions. Isn't it obvious?"

"Treat me like I am four years old and know nothing and tell me why, then," Seon said, quickly losing patience.

At that, Azoz gave Seon a long look. As with many things, it seemed to have dawned on Azoz that Seon did not actually know much about his world. Azoz cocked the half-smile that frustrated Seon so much and then sat down on a log.

"Well, for one thing, a person can do a much more accurate spell on someone with a name," Azoz said, as if Seon should have worked that part out for himself. "It's not necessary though."

"Right," Seon said, sitting down next to Azoz on the log.

He decided not to ask why. He wasn't even sure what Seon meant by a spell. Azoz and Corin had mentioned spells several times without actually teaching Seon any, though he knew how to do basic household chores. He could clean dishes and brush his teeth. Using herbs to heal wounds was still beyond him.

"Naturally the more you know, the more you can direct it," Azoz continued.

Seon just nodded. "So there were more of you then, in the city. The ones who attacked you? Attacked us? They shot you with some kind of spell?"

"In a way," Azoz said.

"What, like with a magic wand or a blaster or something?" Seon said.

At that, Azoz made a noise that was between a grunt and a laugh, "no one uses wands anymore."

"Why not?" Seon asked.

"Too obvious, for one thing," Azoz said. "Also, it's mostly a kid thing. Little kids use them to learn how to focus their magic. Sometimes really old people use a staff. Honestly though, it's a waste."

"Okay," Seon said. "That's why neither of you use one."

"Neither do you," Azoz said. "You've never needed one."

"I can barely do anything," Seon said with a scoff.

"You're too undisciplined," Azoz said, nodding.

"Ha, and you are?" Seon was not sure what else to say to that.

"Maybe," Azoz responded. "Much less than you."

"Well, you have a mentor training you," Seon said, almost thoughtfully. "You can keep him though."

Azoz seemed to find that funny. "You'll get one of your own," he said, getting up off the log and heading towards the woods.

Seon followed Azoz, and the two walked in companionable silence. As usual, after they began walking Alix showed up. This time she perched herself on Seon's wrist. While they walked, Seon realized he probably never would really figure Azoz out completely. It didn't matter. As annoying as he was, it was nice having someone his age to talk to sometimes.

"So, what name will you choose?" Azoz asked after they had been walking for a while.

"I was thinking 'Jaysen,'" Seon said.

"You don't think too much of yourself, do you?" Azoz said with a smirk.

"No," Seon said. "I don't consider myself a hero or anything. It's just that I am an outsider, and Jaysen was an outsider. He had a job to do, and so do I. Maybe if I take his name, I will accomplish mine too."

"Ahh, so taking the name is aspirational," Azoz said.

"I guess so," Seon said.

"Very well ... Jaysen," Azoz said, his voice neither sincere nor kidding. "You can be the one to tell Corin."

Seon wondered if that meant he needed to ask permission, and then decided that would be silly. It was his name after all. He looked out at the still-rising sun, and thought about that. He was still unsure if changing his name was what he really wanted. He wasn't even sure if he wanted to be here at all.

Seon thought about that for a moment, and realized it was going to take awhile for him to even think of himself with his new name. He was in a strange country, where nothing looked like it had back home. That should help. He had already gotten used to the countryside and forests instead of skyscrapers and city streets. Where he came from, trees didn't come in such bright colors though. Flowers were in pinks and purples, and maybe yellows and reds. The trunks of trees tended to be browns and the leaves were more likely to be hues of green, and just a little flashier. They didn't come in neon blue. It was nice to be able to breathe deeply.

"When is Corin coming back?" Seon asked.

"He comes and goes," Azoz answered.

"I'd worked that out for myself, thanks," Seon said.

"He'll return when he does," Azoz said.

Deciding to give it up for now, Seon focused on looking for

plants. He sent Alix off hunting. Seon had enough on his mind and figured it was better to be collecting instead of just walking. There were more than enough along the path. He found morels, tubers, and some edible flowers as well as some herbs. There were plenty of berries and, after determining that they were edible, he dried them and put them in the sack. Drying berries was becoming second nature to him.

Azoz went off hunting and came back with two rabbits, which he skinned and cleaned. Seon dried the meat, a chore he found less pleasant by far than berry drying. He knew it had to be done though. Azoz added some salt to the meat and put it in a sort of spelled leather pouch he carried for the purpose. Seon was tired from the efforts and took a sip from his waterskin. He was just about to suggest a rest when he realized that Aron was frozen, as he always did when he thought there was trouble nearby.

Closing his eyes, Seon tried to close in on the animals around them. It was his ability to sense disruptions in nature that allowed him to know when there was trouble. He wasn't quite sure how Azoz did it. He used his training and his ability to pick up on something. And something was definitely coming. Seon could sense it, now that he knew to look.

"What is it?" he whispered to Azoz.

Even though he could tell that something was wrong, he was not yet sufficiently experienced, trained, or disciplined enough to tell what. There seemed to be something coming toward them, or maybe more than one something. The animals to the northeast of them were scattering or going to ground. It wasn't something big and it wasn't an animal. That was all he could tell.

"Highwaymen, most likely," Azoz said. "Four, maybe more. Coming from the north."

Nodding, Seon looked in that direction. He couldn't sense what the men were thinking. In his head, he was reviewing fighting stances and anything else he had used that could help him. Corin had taught him some of the basics and he had sparred with Azoz dozens of times. These daily fights had gotten him used to the feeling of using what was around him. What he wasn't used to yet was the adrenaline of a fight to come.

"Tell me what to do," Seon said.

It seemed best to give in to Azoz's superior ability and experience here, especially since the opponent was human and not an animal. Seon was better at fighting animals because he could manipulate them and knew what they would do, to a certain extent. It didn't work the same way with people, who were far more complex in their emotions and decision-making.

"Flank me," Azoz said. "And back me up."

Chapter 12

The two came up to the bank of the road slowly, where there was a windbreak of tall bushes that they could hide behind after stashing their packs. They were not able to get too close to the bushes because they were bristling with sharp leaves to protect shiny, steel-colored fruit the size of small plums. Under normal circumstances, Seon would have checked to see if they were edible. He had other things on his mind now.

Luckily the dense tree-like bushes were almost two feet from the ground with tall stalks, so they were able to shimmy under them to watch who was coming. Seon saw that Azoz had been right. There were four scruffy looking men with tanned blue-gray skin and hats pulled down low over their heads, otherwise dressed much as Azoz and Seon were, coming up the road in a loose diamond formation. Had they been back home in his world, he wouldn't expect them to see him hiding under the bushes. Here though, he had learned to assume nothing. He could not tell by looking at the men if they had magic or not. Seon looked over at Azoz. He shook his head.

At first, Seon was not sure what the head-shake meant. It could mean that the men were no threat, or that they should not move. Seon's questioning look had not really been specific enough, and they did not know each other well enough to have nonverbal communication. Neither of them dared enough to speak. Seon knew he didn't, and he doubted Azoz would.

There was suddenly an abrupt change in the energy of the group that Seon did sense. The leader must have been the man in front, because he stopped and said something sharply to the man to his right. Then he looked right at the line of bushes where

Seon and Azoz were hiding. Seon felt his heartrate quicken, even though he was doing his best not to take a breath or let it show. Azoz did not move, but his eyes were intently watching the men. Seon felt hopeless. Before, he had been able to make the group invisible, but it didn't seem to be working now.

While they had magic, Seon and Azoz were not without weapons. They each had an eversharp knife in a sheath in their boot, and another in their jackets. Most formidable in their arsenal was their unique Gifts, however. They had each worked together enough and fought with and against each other enough to have an idea how to use those powers. At least, Seon hoped so.

Without saying a word, Seon closed his eyes and tried to concentrate on the area around them. The men's energy was sufficiently malevolent to have sent the local fauna scattering. Seon had to stretch out behind them farther than usual in order to find what he was looking for.

Off in the distance there was a pack of some kind of mid-sized carnivore. From their intelligence, Seon would have compared them to wolves or panthers, though the mentality was neither canine nor feline. After reaching out and 'listening' in on their consciousness for a few moments, Seon sent them impressions that food was in the direction of the highwaymen. His hope was that the beasts would get the hint and head in the direction of the marauders, giving the men something to fear or at least a distraction. He kept his concentration focused on both parties, trying to sense whether it was working.

Seon was so focused on his inner senses that he almost didn't see what was happening right beside him. Azoz was creeping slowly away from him under the bushes in the direction of the men, knife in hand. Seon saw him finger his medallion quickly, without removing the amethyst that lay within. As he crawled on his belly, Seon opened his eyes. The men were closer now, nearly upon them, while the wolf-cat creatures were coming fast but still too far off to be useful. Seon could barely see what the people were doing, as his attention was focused on the animals, but they looked like rough characters.

Never wishing more that he would communicate telepathically with someone, Seon crawled behind Azoz. They were outnumbered, but numbers might not matter as much as skill level. Seon knew that some magic users could identify others, but it was a specialized ability that not many had. So there was no way to know what these men could do, and Seon was terrified. He was also worried that he was going to do something stupid and get in the way while Azoz was trying to fight.

The best way Seon could contribute to the fight was to bring that pack into it and direct them as his weapons. On his own, Seon was still a mediocre fighter without much confidence, even though he'd once managed to distract Azoz with his Gift. Whether or not he could do that here would depend on the minds of these men. If there was a weak-willed one among them, he might be able to turn that one.

Since Azoz was still crawling toward the road, Seon followed. He tried to split his concentration between the pack and the men. Although he had practiced controlling groups of animals, he always found it difficult to split his concentration this way and he had never succeeded in doing it in a battle. More of his focus was always with the animals and getting them to do what he needed them to do. Being inside an animal's mind was not like seeing the world from a human's perspective, so thinking like a human and an animal at the same time was disorienting.

Communicating with Azoz and controlling the animals to get them to do what he wanted was not easy. He usually ended up speaking to Azoz in gestures or words that made little sense. Their shorthand during a battle with Seon controlling animals just wasn't that coherent yet. He could communicate with Alix much more easily, but she wasn't here. He sent her a quick call, hoping she would return and help, but she was still young and there wouldn't be much she could do when they were so far outnumbered.

They had reached the road now. The men had stopped, and Seon could feel the hunger of the pack. They were close enough now to smell the men as their scent carried on the breeze. One, the leader, let out a carnivorous howl. One of the men in the back of the formation heard, and said something to the others. They stopped, looking around and closing ranks. Their attention was now divided between the bushes and the direction of the howl.

Seon was certain that they knew there were threats from two directions now, but not exactly what they were. They spoke amongst themselves in hurried, disturbed voices. Seon did not understand the words, and he looked at Azoz to see if he did. By the expression on his face, Azoz knew what they were saying. He was listening intently but did not seem concerned. The men were clearly arguing about what to do, but that was all that Seon got from the exchange. He looked a question at Azoz, who shook his head with the smallest gesture. Seon nodded just as minutely. They would wait.

After what felt like much too long to Seon, the group broke up. Half of them headed to one side of the ride, and the other half headed toward the bushes where Seon and Azoz were hiding. Fortunately, this happened just in time for them to take action. At the same time that Azoz popped up from under the bushes, Seon's pack came careening over the other side of the embankment.

Seon barely had a chance to see what they looked like. It was all bright fur and chaos for the time being, so he decided to stay where he was. He knew from experience that trying to get into the fight would be more of a hindrance to Azoz than a help to him. From his vantage point in the dirt, he could see the fight and direct his pack without being in the middle of the fray. Azoz propelled himself into the closest opponent and stabbed him in the chest with an electrified knife, using both his superior fighting skills and his Gift. The man flailed back in surprise and then dropped to the ground, unmoving.

Since Azoz had the element of surprise only once, Seon made the most of the fact that he had his. He urged the feline-esque wolves to see the men as a threat to their territory and acknowledge Azoz as one of their pack. For the most part, they left Azoz alone. The predators were more intelligent than Seon was used to and had some sentience of their own, since being inside their minds was not as easy as he was used to. They seemed confused by his presence and he could not direct them all at once, so he had to identify the alpha and focus on it. Once that was done, he used the alpha to direct his pack to the men who were attacking Azoz, since he was currently fighting off two opponents.

The process was far from foolproof. Azoz had taken some hits, and so had the pack. There were even some friendly fire incidents that Seon had apparently missed while inside the animals' consciousness. When he withdrew, he noticed that there were some animals with singed fur from Azoz's shots at the men and Azoz had a few scratches from claws or teeth. All in all though, for a ferocious fight it seemed to be in their favor.

Unfortunately, directing a pack of animals was tiring work, and Seon's energy was flagging fast. Azoz was drawing energy from reserves Seon did not seem to have, but he was much more injured than Seon was. Neither of them were going to last much longer if Seon did not do something. Without making much of a conscious decision, he jumped up out of his hiding place under the bushes as soon as the alpha was within sight. Bounding over to the creature, he jumped up on its back, linked with its mind, and charged it forward.

This experience was completely different than before. Rather than making suggestions, Seon was communicating, not with words, but with telepathic suggestions, on a one to one level. He used images and feelings that the creature could understand because he had been inside its mind for the past twenty minutes and understood how it thought and felt. It was time to end this.

Seon and Alpha had one common goal. They both wanted to end the fight and stop the threat. The men were hurting the pack. Both of them wanted them stopped. Seon let Alpha know that Azoz was a friend. He was trying to protect the pack. The men were trying to hurt them. Alpha was confused, because he was not used to having someone ride him. He allowed it because the rider was in his mind.

It was at this point in the battle that Alix returned. She must have been far away. She began pecking at the men and screeching, flying around and flapping her wings and generally causing chaos. Her arrival could not have come at a better time. She was just enough of a distraction to help Azoz and Seon's pack finish them off.

With Seon and Alpha working together, they made short work of the rest of the men. Azoz had been holding his own pretty well, and he had done a good job weakening his opponents although he was outnumbered as far as humans were concerned. Alpha had the rest of the men down, even though some of them were still moaning and moving. Azoz went up to one of them and stabbed him in the heart. Seon watched this, unsure how he felt about it. It seemed like such a final action. These men were their enemy only because they were fighting them. Other than that, they knew nothing at all about them.

There was little time for moral quandaries though. Seon jumped down from Alpha, sliding down blood-slicked white-gray fur as the creature dropped to its belly and began licking its wounds. Two of the pack were dead, and the rest of the seven creatures were all wounded to varying levels of intensity. Some even looked as though they might have been pecked. Seon gulped, seeing that one of the creatures was singed in the eye. He would have to ask Azoz about that later.

For the most part, however, the men they had fought were much worse off. Half of them were dead or dying. The other three were laying on the ground in various states of pain. They were covered in knife wounds, burn marks, hawk-pecks, and bite marks. Azoz grabbed one man by the leg and dragged him unceremoniously over to one of the others. He then reached into his pockets and withdrew a leather cord, tied the man's hands, and then did the same with his feet. Seon decided that he might as well help and hauled one of the other men to his feet. The man was next to unconscious and mumbling, so Seon half carried him as gently as he could over to where the others were and then laid him down. He returned to the bushes where their packs were, wishing he had planned ahead like Azoz had. It didn't take him long to find the cord, cut it with his knife, and tie up his prisoner as well. By the time he had done that, Azoz had the third injured man in the group and hogtied.

"Well," Seon said, looking around at the carnage. "What do we do now?"

The pack was lounging around in the closest thing that passed for shade near some trees. None of them were looking at Seon or Azoz, and Seon had sent them impressions that the boys were harmless. They all had wounds to lick and were exhausted. Seon was hoping that they were too tired to bother anyone. He empathized more and more with animals and felt terrible for having used them the way he had when he saw them laying dead and wounded. Underneath the fur, hair tanned blue-gray color, scaly skin was fading fast.

There were now more pressing concerns though. Not all of their attackers were dead. Two of them were conscious, and as Seon was staring at the creatures who had fought for him, one of the men they had fought had been shouting angry invective at Azoz. Although Azoz was currently ignoring him and standing in front of him with his arms at his sides in a posture that Seon had come to learn meant he was annoyed, Seon was nervous. He had never killed anyone before. Two men were dead, two were seriously injured, and two were prisoners. Seon had no idea what they were going to do.

"Azoz," Seon whispered, trying not to be too much of a distraction.

Without looking at Seon, Azoz said something in the same language the man had been speaking. Seon barely recognized his tone. It was forceful and did not sound like it belonged to a teen. The voice was hard and cold, but whatever he said also stopped the man's diatribe. He looked at Seon, then the pack, and then said nothing.

Seon felt suddenly sickened. He had an idea that he knew exactly what Azoz had said. He wasn't happy with the implication, but it really made no difference. If the men were more afraid of him than Azoz, it made no difference. They needed compliance.

Azoz made a slight scoffing sound and then walked in no hurry over to Seon. While he had wanted to talk to Azoz before, Seon was not sure what to say now. He felt surprisingly alone. He had come to rely on Azoz over the short time they had spent together, and even saw him as a friend in some ways. Now he was seeing him, and the journey, in a different light. It was more than serious. It was deadly.

"They are not a threat," Azoz said, his voice low and almost toneless. "We took out the stronger ones first."

Deciding not to bring up the issue of 'first,' Seon instead chose to focus on what he saw as the bigger problem. "What are we going to do now?"

"I should think that's obvious," Azoz said, giving Seon a look that implied what he thought of the question.

"No, it's not," Seon said. "Are they really a threat to us? Like you said, they are just highwaymen. Robbers, right? Do they even have magical abilities?" At the shake of Azoz's head, Seon found himself getting more frustrated. "We can't just kill them. It's murder."

"What do you suggest?" Azoz asked cooly.

"Can't we just leave them here?" Seon asked. "Tie them up. Move on. Eventually they get out, but we will be long gone. Do you really think they are going to come after us?"

The two stared at each other for a few moments. Finally, Azoz nodded. Seon felt relieved, but it did not seem like a victory. It was still a lot of carnage for what seemed like no reason.

They picked up their packs and began walking. Once they had covered enough ground, Seon sent a compulsion back to the pack to stay for a while and then leave. It should give them plenty of time. They had both retrieved all of their gear and were on the other side of the road, down the embankment, moving at a fast pace that was not actually running.

"Do you have some way of communicating with Corin?" Seon asked.

"Sort of," Azoz said.

"What is that supposed to mean?" Seon demanded. He was getting tired of half-answers and limited information from these two.

"It means 'sort of,'" Azoz said, without stopping. "He knows when I am in trouble. He knows that I am no longer in danger. He knows the general direction I am headed."

"How?" Seon asked.

Azoz directed an uninterpretable look at Seon. "Magic."

If it had not been for the fact that Azoz could flatten him with one hand, Seon would have been very tempted to sock him. There was little point though. Seon was never going to get any more out of him. As frustrating as Azoz was, at least he was consistent.

The two continued walking until the dusk got so thick that they could no longer see. Then Azoz made a stew that Seon well knew had bits of rabbit in it, but he didn't care. He was tired of fighting for the day, and that included fighting Azoz. When he fell asleep, he was thinking of Emili and wondering what she was doing.

It wasn't long before he was dreaming of her.

Emili ... Please tell me where you are so I can get to you. I don't know how much more of this I can take. Seon begged.

He could see her, fuzzy as always. There was a vague sense of long, plaited hair. He could not see her face. Her eyes were missing. They were there of course, and he could tell she was watching him imperatively, but he could not see her face. The usual interference was there.

Wanting to cry out in frustration, Seon decided to try another tactic. Instead, he reached out into the landscape around her and focused. He was still better with plants and animals than people, in terms of getting a reading and a feel. He could sense a body of water. It was smaller than a river but it wasn't pooled like a lake. It was moving, and not deep. It was a stream or a brook. There were animals, and quite a few. Their minds showed a sense of domestication. It was a farm. She was on a farm. Reaching out wider, he sensed the consciousness of more feral animals and what he had come to associate with trees. It was not sentience of any kind, but it was more of a presence. It was a forest.

She was on a farm, near a forest. There was more though. In the other direction, he could sense a buzzing that meant a village or a small town. He had felt it when they had edged close to them, but not within them. The farm was on the outskirts of a village near a forest where there was a small stream. Geographically, those were pretty specific details.

He had found Emili.

Chapter 13

Seon was excited to tell Azoz what he had found when he woke up the next morning. For some reason, he had not woken up right after his encounter with Emili in the dream. He had continued to sleep for several hours more. He supposed his body had been so exhausted that he had just passed out from the effort. Either way, there was no other option but to continue on. Apparently, willing himself awake wasn't his choice.

When his eyes did open, Azoz was nowhere to be seen. At first, Seon thought nothing of it. Then, he became a little worried as the dawn stretched into day and his traveling companions were nowhere to be found. It was unusual for him to be left alone. At first, they were probably just worried he couldn't fend for himself. It wasn't like he could run away. There was nowhere for him to go. He didn't speak any of the languages and he didn't understand the customs. His ability to defend himself and his magic was rudimentary. At least Alix had not deserted him. His feathered friend remained steadfastly by his side.

It was with a sense of frustration that Seon began to pack up and set off to look for food. He decided that foraging for berries was the best use of his time. He could always return to the clearing later, or wait for Azoz to find him. Even if Azoz had some kind of weird connection with Corin, it did not mean that he and Seon had the same kind of connection. On the contrary, they came from different worlds and barely understood each other. Seon was starting to think he might not want to. As carefree and silly as Azoz could be, he was also ruthless. Sometimes Seon had trouble reconciling the two sides of him.

For the next hour or so, Seon picked herbs and berries and thought of little else. He kept his eyes out for predators and looked at the landscape. They were no longer in constant forests. Now there was tundra as far as the eye could see, with scrubby bushes and islands of trees breaking up the monotony and offering shelter for the animal population. The animals consisted of small game and wolven creatures, and the temperature was colder. Seon realized that his gear seemed to adapt to varying weather, and he was comfortable now just as he had been in the warmer conditions.

After a while, Seon decided it didn't matter to him whether or not Azoz showed up. He had a general direction to head, and more importantly a destination. He did not know the name of the town, and couldn't speak the language to ask anyone directions, but he knew essentially what he was looking for. He was confident that he would know the farm when he found it. He would know when he found *her*.

It seemed like Seon walked for hours. He stopped only to eat some of the berries he had collected or take more if he saw something worthy of adding to his small stores. He was no longer gathering for three, but mainly taking enough for himself. If he made it to the village where Emili was on his own, so much the better. He had wanted to meet her before they came to get him. It didn't matter that they kidnapped him and essentially forced him along, he didn't know the language, and he wasn't sure where he was going. Seon was doing this on his own.

After what seemed like days of walking, Seon came to a small hamlet. This was the real test for him. He knew that he could not go in, because he would not be able to talk to anyone. So he camped outside. For the first time, he wondered where Azoz was. It occurred to him that Azoz might have gone to meet up with

Corin. It was not usual at all for Corin to disappear, and Seon had not seen Azoz's mentor in days. At this point he thought it was better that he didn't. Seon steered clear of the place and that night he settled down and camped in a hollowed out space made by a fallen tree trunk and slept fitfully. He did feel safer when he had backup.

The next morning, he awoke before dawn broke. He could see the very beginning of the sunrise against a tiny swath of forest in the distance. He was aiming for that forest. First, he needed to find water. His supply was dangerously low since he had used most of it up in the last two days. Seon headed east, since he felt instinctively that there was water that way. His instincts had not been wrong yet.

It turned out to be a pond and not a stream. Seon walked around it until he found the stream that fed into it. He checked the water with a spell Azoz had shown him and then filled his waterskins, drank from one greedily but not so much he would be sick, and filled that one again. He saw some edible plants in the water and made himself a small vegetarian stew. It was tasty with the herbs and edible flowers he had collected, and he sat in the shade of the stream even though the weather was cool.

After he was finished, he cleaned his cup and pot and returned to the road. Just like when he had traveled with Azoz, he wasn't walking on the road or even along it. He could see it from where he was though, and tried to keep it in sight while also keeping cover. It wasn't a well traveled road, even though he had passed the village. The people who did use the road seemed to be minding their own business. Seon had seen no sign of technology anywhere. There were no vehicles that weren't drawn by animals.

Since he knew he was headed in the right direction, Seon decided to try to find Emili again. He wondered if he could do it without sleeping. Finding a sheltered swatch of trees, Seon nestled himself against a tree, sitting cross-legged. Alix settled down on a tree stump next to him, as if keeping watch.

Seon reached down deep into himself and tried to find a center of calm. It was not easy to do when his mind was racing with questions and confusion. Eventually, however, he settled into a sense of calm and quieted his mind. Then he tried to reach out to her.

Emili. I am here. I am close. Where are you?

At first, there was no response to Seon's calls. Then he felt a gentle pulling sensation, almost like a breeze, in the direction to the east. It felt familiar, and he knew it was her. Emili was calling back to him, and although he did not hear her response in words, he could sense it as clearly as if she were standing next to him talking. He tried again.

Please, tell me where you are.

Again, he could sense her. Since he was still in a trance, he was not sure what she was trying to say or where she was. Instead of words, he got a sense of impressions. They were clearer this time, but not as clear as when he was asleep. He had a hazy image of waving grains in a field, the brook he had deduced must be there, and a wide expanse of dense, jungle-like forest. Those were the trees he could see in the distance. He was so close.

The connection was lost. Seon slowly returned to his awareness of the world around him, and looked out into the distance to see the trees. He couldn't believe that he was so close. After months of seeing her and wondering if she was real, and then days of endless walking and putting up with Azoz and Corin, here he was, alone, at the edge of a forest in a world he barely knew and understood even less. He was going to find her. He was going to see her. Emili was there.

With newfound resolve, Seon made his way across the harsh landscape. The wind was biting cold against his face. He might not have felt it anywhere else, because of the excellent gear he had been given, but the constant barrage against his eyes was getting to him. There was little refuge to be found amongst the scrubby bushes, even if he was interested in stopping to rest. Seon was singularly focused on that treeline.

The nearness of the trees turned out to be an illusion. After walking for most of a day, Seon felt that he was no closer than he had been when he started. While that certainly could not be true, he definitely wasn't in the forest. It remained elusive and frustratingly out of reach. When he made camp that night amongst a cluster of rocks and bushes, it still looked tantalizingly close. Seon knew better. It almost seemed as though while he was walking toward the forest, it was walking away from him.

After sleeping fretfully that night, Seon woke up sore and tired. The journey was getting to him. He even missed Azoz's wisecracks. Talking to Alix did not give him the same satisfaction as a person would, apparently.

"No offense, Alix," Seon said out loud, reaching out to stroke the bird's feathers gently.

Alix tossed her head as if she understood. Seon wondered idly if she felt the same way. She might get lonely for other hawks, if she hadn't found some magical hawks to make friends with along their travels. Seon knew he was feeling very desperate if he missed Azoz's company.

Seon knew that in order to reach the forest in any reasonable amount of time, he was going to need to walk at a good pace with few breaks. There was no way to pass the time other than to talk to Alix, when she wasn't off hunting. Most of the time she stayed close, something he was grateful for. The wind whipped at his face and he wondered idly to himself if he preferred heat or wind. It made little sense to him that the landscape he saw in his visions could reconcile with this one. Those trees had seemed lush and green, like a rainforest. The tundra was harsh and bleak, and did not make him think of a place teeming with life or warmth.

The other problem was that he felt exposed. There was hardly any cover out here. Every once in a while there were large rocks or groups of bushes or grubby trees that had managed to grow taller despite the crushing winds. Overall, though, it was just grass, short scrub brush, and not much else. There was nowhere to hide. Alix kept close to Seon and he was grateful for more than her company. He kept his senses alert almost constantly, watchful for animals and people alike. Any kind of foe out here would be dangerous.

The trouble Seon had been fearing came to pass near dusk on his third day alone. He had already been seeking out shelter when he started to sense that he was being followed. He could tell that it wasn't entirely human, but it didn't appear to be an animal either. The consciousness seemed almost reptilian, but it wasn't anything that he had felt before. He would not know the creature if he saw it, he was sure. Nonetheless, his head jerked around as quickly as possible in all directions, looking for the threat.

At first, he did not see anything. It was getting closer and closer to darkness, and the animal could be blending in. Then, at the edge of his consciousness, he felt a tickle. It was almost as if the animal had felt him and was trying to push him back or inquire as to his presence. The sensation was so unusual that Seon withdrew, confused and repulsed. Its presence was oily and cold-blooded, and definitely not human.

Without making a noise, Seon called out to Alix. She came closer and hovered over him, but did not land. They both faced off in the direction of the creature without moving toward it or away. Seon knew that he had given away his presence and there was no way to take shelter or hide. It wasn't like when he and Azoz had fought the highwaymen. There was no cover here on the tundra.

Since there was no alternative, Seon stood his ground. He glared into the distance against the biting cold and watched as a large red-orange reptilian creature came lumbering toward him. He noticed that it did seem to have some kind of fur covering its back and its legs and it was low to the ground but huge, closer to the size of a small hippopotamus.

When the creature was close enough, he was able to see that it was not hair. The creature had rows of tiny spikes going down the middle of its back and down its front and back legs that had looked like spongy hair from a distance. The spikes were a burnt orange color like sunset, whereas the creature itself was more auburn. Its scaly skin was thick and callused.

In all of his fights, Seon had never fought on his own one to one against an animal opponent. When he had fought against an animal and tried to manipulate it, it been a disaster. The last time he had fought and used animals he had left the fight feeling miserable, as if he had violated the sanctity of life and misused his gift, even though he and Azoz had survived. They had killed those men even though they hadn't really known their motives or even who they were.

Now it was clearly kill or be killed. He could sense it in the animal's consciousness. It didn't even want to eat Seon, necessarily. It wanted to kill him and then see if he would make good food. This animal enjoyed killing. It had enough sentience to hunt for fun. Like mankind, it enjoyed the thrill of the fight.

Seon had no such thrill from the kill. He did not enjoy fighting or even sparring. He felt some satisfaction from healing and was looking forward to becoming an apprentice and learning to use his magic for more than just winning fights. Senseless killing did not excite him. Fighting for fun was not his thing. He knew Azoz seemed to enjoy it and Azoz was good at it, maybe because of that. Seon doubted he would ever be a good fighter and he did not have Azoz's natural talent.

While all of this was going through his head, he tried to remember everything Azoz had taught him and Corin had drilled into him. There was a lot to remember, and he knew that at some point instinct and practice was going to need to take over. The creature was taking too long. He might be enjoying making Seon squirm.

It certainly seemed like it.

Carefully, Seon withdrew from the consciousness of the monster, as Seon now thought of him. He wanted to go at this from a different angle. He tried to leave without a trace, so that creature would not know it. That way what he was planning would be more of a surprise. If Seon was going to win, he needed to fight with everything he had. Seon's magic was his best weapon.

You take him from above, Seon said, nuding the thought to Alix gently with his mind. *I'm going to make him think I'm weak.*

It would not be a hard sell. The creature was huge, weighing many times more than Seon even with the amount of muscle he was slowly adding. More importantly, the closer it got, Seon could see the large claws on its toes. Its defensive weapons made his knives seem paltry. It wasn't as if he could electrify his weapons the way Azoz could.

When the creature was within calling distance of Seon, had they spoken the same language, it stopped. He stared it down, hoping that he was not showing any outward signs of intimidation. Alix was well above him, staying out of sight. She would come when the time was right.

Neither advanced. Confident that it was waiting for him to make the first move, Seon took a deep breath and reached inside himself for that calm center that was eluding him. He was not all that interested in closing his eyes in front of this creature, but that was how he usually meditated. So he relaxed, closed his eyes, and realized that he still knew where everything was even without his eyes open. His senses were just as strong. In some ways, he felt more aware. His eyes made him fear. His calm center made him focus.

You do not want to fight me.

There was a reaction. It wasn't in words, but it was a reaction all the same. Seon would have roughly translated it as, "No, I do not want to fight you. I want to kill you and see if I should eat you." Well, that he could work with.

You do not want to eat me. I am too small. There is no meat on my bones. I do not taste good.

Disbelief was the response. Seon had to admit, he had no way of knowing how he would taste. He could clearly show that he had no meat on his bones though. That was obvious. He continued, this time with stronger suggestions.

You. Do. Not. Want. To. Fight.

You. Do. Not. Want. To. Eat. Me.

I. Taste. Bad.

I. Am. Not. Enough.

He repeated this mantra over and over. Eventually he began to get the impression that it was working. The sense that he was getting from the creature was confusion, or maybe even dizziness. Seon wished he knew what the creature called itself. Azoz had said that there was power in names. If he knew its name, maybe he could cast this spell. 'Ugly beast' probably would not work.

Now, Alix, he thought.

She came diving out of the sky, from so high up that he hadn't even seen her himself. Although she was young, she was smart and she had the benefit of her connection with him. She targeted its weak spots. Since Seon wasn't sure what else to go for, they went for the obvious.

She gouged at its eyes.

In a way, Seon was glad that his own eyes were closed. To see the attack through his limited perception of Alix's senses was bad enough. He didn't want to see it with his own eyes. He was directing it, and he was somewhat sensing it from their prey. He could feel it from both sides.

The attack was only a diversion. As soon as Alix began her divebomb, Seon began his charge.

Chapter 14

With Alix distracting the lizard-monster, Seon went in for the kill. He was all business. This was not the time for philosophical debate or self-doubt. Too many things could go wrong if he hesitated, because everything depended on split second-timing and trusting his instincts. He could see through Alix's eyes, and sense through the creature's senses. As soon as he got close enough to smell it, he let go of Alix's perception and focused in on his own, trying his best not to get disoriented by the shift from hawk-sense to human-sense.

It smelled horrible, and up close it was so big that Seon almost lost his nerve. The monster towered over him, but he ignored that. He knew that given its scaly skin and spines, it would be better to look for a soft underbelly anyway. His small size might be to his advantage—as long as it didn't crush him to death.

Seon did not want to jump up on its back because of the spikes. He wasn't so sure of his grip on the knife through the leather gloves. They were strong, even though they were thin. He definitely needed to wear them. He wished he had tried more knife-in-glove practice. There was no time for wishing now though. He was just going to have to try for brute force and hope that the magical knives did the trick against a magical beast.

Running through his inventory of Gifts in his head, Seon relied on the only other one he could use in this situation. He had his gear, his knife, and his bird currently gouging out the eyes of the beast, which was thrashing around trying to throw her off.

Stop!

Seon put as much force into the command as he could. He put all of his energy and will into it, throwing himself at the underside of the beast and ramming his knife at what he hoped would be an internal organ. If his animal sense was true, it would find one.

It worked. The knife found an organ. Seon could tell that it was the heart. He knew because he sensed it, through the connection he had to the beast, but also because after a death-jerk, the animal let out a ghastly roar, gurgled, and fell silent in death.

Seon rolled backward quickly, jumping out of the way so as not to get crushed when the beast landed. Alix fluttered down and perched on his shoulder, as if in solidarity. Seon sighed, and sat back. He was so exhausted he was tempted to pass out right there. The sun would set soon though, and he needed to find shelter. The fight had taken the last of his reserves, and he felt as if he could barely move.

Looking around him, he didn't see any trees or rock formations nearby. He didn't feel that it was a good idea to stay anywhere near the slain beast. Scavengers would soon come from everywhere around to pick the carcass clean. He didn't want to be in the position of having to fight them too.

After waiting as long as he felt he could, Seon stood up and started to walk. It wasn't very far before his legs started to feel wobbly under him. Alix made a small noise that seemed to express concern. Seon stopped walking to steady himself.

"It's okay girl," Seon said. "I'm just tired."

When he reached a small outcropping of rocks and trees, Seon stopped and sat down. He felt woozy and his legs seemed no longer able to hold him. Keeping his knife in his hand, he fell into a semi-conscious sleep. How long he remained that way he wasn't sure. Alix was keeping watch, but Seon had a feeling of danger not far off, and was trying to keep himself from falling too deeply in. If he gave in to his drowsiness, all could be lost.

"Can't," he mumbled. "Not now..."

At the far edge of his consciousness, something was creeping closer. It wasn't large like the lizard monster, or a pack, like the canine-felines. This was great in number and hunger, not in size. It was either his imagination, or something was crawling over him.

It wasn't his imagination.

Seon jumped to his feet. Everywhere he looked, there were small insects. They pooled in great swarms, and were so loud it was hurting his ears. He let out a strangled cry of alarm and surprise, brushing them off even as they were still coming. Ants!

The first ones were the size of beetles, and he was able to remove them from his clothing with relative ease. They seemed to be moving past him and over him as if he was just another obstacle in their path. He could see more coming, however, and they were getting bigger and bigger. The next smallest ones were comparable to birds and then they became the size of cats or small dogs. Seon thought about running, but had no idea where to run to. His attempts to manipulate insect hoards had always netted mixed results.

"Azoz, I could really use you now," he said out loud.

While Seon was fighting off the insectes, Alix was dive bombing them, feasting on the smaller ones and impaling the larger ones. Even she had eaten her fill soon enough. They just kept coming.

"Think, Seon," he implored himself.

When he reached out to try to feel inside their consciousness, he was overwhelmed by so many tiny minds. They were alien not just by being from another land, but by thinking like insects.

Their single-mindedness confused him and disoriented him. He couldn't find purchase anywhere.

"This is not working," Seon said.

It occurred to him that if all of the insects were headed in a particular direction, there had to be a reason. They were either headed to something or away from it. Since they were not going toward the carcass of the lizard monster, they might be afraid of what had killed it, or there might be something worse back there. He had killed the monster, and it was pretty formidable. Still, he would hate to see what this throng of insects was afraid of. The biggest ones were frightening to him, but it was more the sheer number of them. Seon had never been fond of large groups of insects, despite his affinity for animals and plants. He disliked ants most of all, as useful as they were in nature.

Deciding not to think about that now, Seon took off running. Under his feet crunched hundreds of the ant-like insects. The sound was horrifying. Since he was still connected to their consciousness at first, he felt their little lights go out. Seon withdrew quickly, and kept running. He was headed in the same direction, even though looking back he didn't see anything to run from. Trusting the masses seemed like the best plan in these circumstances, even though it meant literally running over them.

The problem was that he was going nowhere fast. The critters were streaming under him, and he couldn't get very far. It wasn't long before Seon felt like he was running on a treadmill. It was both frustrating and exhausting. He hadn't rested long and he was still feeling drained. If he fell, he was sure they would just keep running over him, and probably eat him where he lay.

"This isn't working, Alix!" Seon shouted.

For the first time, he wished she were a larger bird. If Alix was big enough, she could just carry him out of this mess. As it was, nothing short of a helicopter was going to rescue him unless he could find a way to part the masses of insects. He needed to get out of the throng, and fast. He pondered the problem, and realized that he could use the fact that these were ants. Ants did not think or make decisions individually. They had a hive mind. They were a collective. He had to influence the queen.

Come on, Seon. You can out-think a bunch of bugs.

Unfortunately it was difficult to concentrate on a treadmill of increasingly large insects. Seon grunted and panted, and tried to focus. He did not want to close his eyes, because he was afraid to lose his footing. At the same time, not seeing what was around him could only be a positive. He had meditated without closing his eyes before, and when he saw through the senses of other creatures, he didn't use his own anyway. So Seon left his eyes open for the time being and withdrew from his own consciousness into the collective consciousness of the ant hive-mind.

It was still a strange sensation, but he was more prepared this time. After he settled in, he sought out the queen. She was nowhere near him, deep in the hollow of the nest. She was concerned, not for herself, but for her 'workers' or 'soldiers." Seon wasn't sure of the exact translation. Something was coming. It was organic, but it wasn't alive. She was afraid for them.

Fire!

It all made sense now. The insects were running from the fire, because somehow the queen knew. There were probably other animals running from the fire too, but they were steering clear of the insects because there were so many of them and some of them were huge. Seon shuddered to think of how large the queen must be. He was glad he could not see her.

With newfound resolve, Seon focused on the queen. He told her to send her hoards of soldiers eastward in columns, rather than swarms. Although the ants were not nearly as disciplined as that, they did begin to bunch together. Seon took advantage of this to make his exit through the ranks. It was a little difficult to focus on keeping the path between teeming rows of insects and his hold on the queen. He concentrated with all his might though, because the alternative was unthinkable.

The problem was that the direction he was heading was overpopulated. The giant ants were not the only ones evacuating the fire. There were animals of all kinds heading in the direction of the forest, and just because they were running from the fire did not mean they were not a threat. If Seon got in their way, they might run him down or attack him even if they were not interested in seeing him as food at the moment. There were too many to manipulate, and Seon was still busy with the ants.

The situation was getting more and more untenable by the moment. Seon had been exhausted when he started, and now he was running on adrenaline. He simply did not have the time to think about tiring. If he stopped, he would be trampled. If he lost his focus, he would die. So he kept running. Alix flew just overhead, screeching every once in a while as if she was encouraging him. Maybe she was just as frustrated and frightened as he was.

There was a great crash from somewhere behind him that sounded like two large beasts were fighting. Seon didn't turn back to look, but the sound broke his concentration and made him lose his footing. Almost in an instant, there was a response from the insects around him, and not the one he wanted. The bugs broke ranks and scattered as Seon lost his hold on the queen, but apparently the law of unintended consequences went both ways. She had lost her hold on them too. Confused and frightened, they ran in all directions. Since there was no real pattern to their flight, Seon was able to power right through them, toward the forest.

It was a good thing too, because he was being followed, or chased, by something huge and malevolent. It looked like a large mammal, about the size of an elephant. It was dark blue or purple, and so tall that he could not clearly see the top of it. Seon groaned, or maybe screamed, and tried to gather up enough strength to run faster.

Instead he fell.

The ground was mucky and full of the footprints of hundreds of animals. The ones that had tripped Seon were as large as his foot, but only just. He reached down and desperately tried to pull his foot out of the hole, but it wouldn't budge. The hole was full of mud and sucking him in like quicksand, so that he was sinking deeper and deeper. He reached down and yanked on his boot, trying to pull his foot out by brute force.

It was no use. His foot was stuck well in his boot, and his boot was stuck well in the hole.

Seon was frantically alternating at pulling at his foot and trying to claw away at the mud surrounding it, but every time he made any progress, the hole just filled back in. He cried out in frustration. The creature was getting closer, and Seon wondered whether it was going to just lumber over him or step on him. The closer it got, the more he started calculating. He decided his best bet was to sink down close to the ground and try to reach out for the creature and tell it to go around him. Once it was past, he would have to get out. Somehow.

Chapter 15

Ducking down, Seon tried to make himself the smallest target possible. He hunched over in a sitting position, since he could not very well lay down with his foot stuck in a hole. Cursing the lack of focus that got him into this position in the first place, he tried to reach out and find the consciousness of the elephantine creature. It was elusive, and not as intelligent as he was expecting. He wasn't sure why he'd thought it would understand more, or he'd be able to understand more of the environment within its consciousness. Size did not equate intelligence in this case. Seon was having a hard time interpreting its senses sufficiently to influence it enough to tell it to leave him alone.

From his position in the mud, and his consciousness deep within the elephant creature, Seon began to think he was hallucinating. Somewhere in the depths of his mind, he thought he heard his name being called. He couldn't imagine who would be calling his name. It must be the imminence of his death. He tried not to think of it, but he was also realistic. Even if this thing didn't get him, something else might.

"Seon!"

He hadn't imagined it. Someone was calling his name. Seon looked up, and around, and tried to hear the voice again. He could not find where the sound was coming from. He decided he must have imagined it.

Then, from behind him, a bolt of energy shot at the beast. At first, it kept lumbering along. Then it seemed to realize it had been hit, and it stopped and fell, first to one knee, and then to the other. Finally, it fell over sideways. The fall came with a tremendous crash. Seon stared at it in disbelief.

"Seon."

There was the voice again. As difficult as it was to believe, it had been real. Seon looked around, and up. From behind the beast he could see Azoz grinning at him.

"That was something else, wasn't it?" said Azoz.

"Azoz," Seon said. "You couldn't have come at a better time."

With a crooked smile, Azoz ran up to Seon and grabbed ahold of his outstretched hand. Azoz was taller and stronger than Seon, but he also had better leverage. He was able to pull Seon out of the muck, but it took some effort even on his part.

"How did you get yourself in this predicament," Azoz demanded, with emphasis on the first word.

"Shouldn't we try to get out of here, and you can lecture me later?" Seon said, looking around anxiously. It couldn't have escaped his notice that there was still a fire and a stampede.

"Oh, the fire?" Azoz said nonchalantly. "Right.'

"Did you start it?" Seon asked.

"Not intentionally," Azoz said.

"Are you crazy?" Seon said. "You could have killed us all, not to mention all these animals."

Azoz shrugged. "What do you want me to say? I didn't do it on purpose. I think it helped us actually. Anyway, it is burning itself out. It won't get to the forest."

"Oh, well, as long as you didn't do it on purpose," Seon said, glaring at Azoz. "Lives lost don't matter to you. I forgot."

"Some lives matter more than others, Seon," Azoz said. "I am not going to apologize for what I did back there. Or what I did here. I just saved your life, in case you missed it."

"Yeah," Seon said. "Thanks."

He started walking, but it was almost impossible. His boots were covered so thickly in mud that he could barely move them.

He stomped his feet as he walked to try to clear some of it, but it was hardly a dignified exit. Eventually, he was more able to walk and the muck settled into a thick cake of dried crud that just made his boots heavier.

"You know," Azoz said after they had been walking a while in silence, "you do pretty well on your own."

"Is that so?" Seon said. "I didn't have much of a choice."

"No, I guess you didn't," Azoz said.

"Where were you?" Seon asked, finally conceding to look at Azoz.

"I had something to do," Azoz said with a shrug. "I got ... waylaid."

"Waylaid?" Seon said incredulously. "You and Corin kidnapped me and forced me to come here. I wasn't expecting to be stranded on my own and have to fend for myself in an alien world."

"Alien?" Azoz asked with a chuckle.

"I don't know this place," Seon reminded him. "I don't speak the language, and the plants and animals are not like mine."

"They must be close enough," Azoz said. "You are doing fine."

"Am I though?" Seon asked. "I almost just got squashed by a purple elephant. You had to save my neck."

"Well, everyone needs help every once in a while," Azoz said. "That's why we work in teams."

"Right," Seon said. "I did not have a team."

"No," Azoz said, then softly added. "Things don't always go as planned."

Having nothing to say to that, Seon just kept on walking. He was getting tireder and tireder as the adrenalin from his second wind ran out. His feet seemed as heavy as bricks. He began to stumble more and more.

Finally, they stopped. Seon was glad, since he could no longer see to walk. The fire must have been out, or they would have seen it in the dark. Seon sat down on a log and Azoz started a fire. Seon was thinking sleepily that it was lucky that there were logs and small pieces of wood in the middle of the tundra, when he realized they must no longer be in the tundra. They were getting closer to the forest, and there were more and more trees. The trees where they were camped were close enough together for cover, and there were enough lying around to make a campfire and a shelter. Seon was grateful for Azoz, because he was too tired to do anything for himself. All he did was take off his boots, and then he was asleep with his pack for a pillow.

"Seon."

"Ugh."

"Seon, wake up!"

"No."

"Come on, Seon, you've been asleep all night, and you need to eat something."

"No."

Seon was barely aware that he was even talking. He wanted to sleep. Somewhere he was conscious of the fact that he was, indeed, hungry, but he was tired deep in his bones. He could not force his eyes to open.

"Seon," Azoz said again, more insistent this time. "Do you really want me to waste the contents of this waterskin by pouring it over your head?"

"Would you?" Seon asked, not opening his eyes.

"Yes," Azoz said.

From the tone of his voice, Seon did not doubt that he would, so he opened his eyes and slowly sat up. He had a bone-crushing pain in his left-leg and a stabbing pain in his head. That was on top of an aching, throbbing, pain that radiated from every joint in his body.

"I think I broke something," Seon said.

"You might have," Azoz agreed. "Eat, and then you can heal yourself."

"Shouldn't we move first?" Seon asked. "Go to shelter?"

"We're fine here for another day, or part of one," Azoz said with a shrug. You're in no condition to move. Your ankle is sprained, your wrist is broken, and I have no idea what you did to your eyes."

"My eyes?"

"I wish you could see yourself," Azoz said.

"Never mind," Seon did not want to look.

He did have a headache, but he realized it was more than that. It hurt to open his eyes. The pain came from the eyes themselves, as well as his head. He decided against asking what they looked like, for now. Hopefully, he would be able to fix himself.

"Are you hurt?" Seon asked, squinting and trying to look up at Azoz.

"Minor scrapes and bruises," Azoz said with a shrug. "Nothing that won't go away on its own. I have some herbs and tinctures."

Seon nodded. He put his head back down and sighed. Food, then healing. A half a day would have to be enough. He simply did not have the energy to heal himself and then Azoz, at least for now. Out of the corner of his eye he noticed that Azoz wasn't much more active than he was. He was leaning against a tree with his amethyst in his hand, most likely meditating.

The rest of the day Seon spent in a meditation induced fog as he tried to heal his injuries despite his exhaustion. It worked better when he wasn't short on sleep and nutrients and when there weren't so many injuries to heal. He did his best, and by the late afternoon he felt that he could walk.

When Azoz handed him a stone tumbler with a hearty stew full of chunks of meat, tubers, morels, and herbs, Seon didn't even protest. He was simply too hungry and spent. While he detested eating animals, he knew that he needed protein and his body needed sustenance. Azoz had filled the stew with as many healing herbs as he could, and Seon could feel it going to work as soon as he took the first sip.

"Better?" Azoz asked. For once there was no sarcasm or jest in his voice, only concern.

"Yeah," Seon said. "It's been a rough few days."

"I noticed," Azoz said. "I cleaned your boots."

At that pronouncement, Azoz held up Seon's boots. Somehow they looked as good as new. Azoz had not only scraped the mud off of them, he had oiled them and dug mud out of the treads. It would be much easier to walk now. As a peace offering, it was a start.

"Thanks," Seon said. "Better than I could've done.'

Grinning, Azoz tossed the boots at Seon none too gently. They were loosely knotted together at the laces. Seon picked them up, untied them and started to put them on. They were as comfortable as ever, buttery soft and molded to his feet. He wasn't sure if it was the spells woven into the leather or the fact that they were just really-well made shoes. It was probably a combination of both.

After checking his boots over for damage, Seon looked at the rest of his gear. Like Azoz, he now had a collection of scrapes and nicks. It had held up surprisingly well, however, and considering what he had been through over the past few days he had expected more. The jacket still covered and the pack was still together. All in all, Seon was impressed.

"Yep," Azoz said. "You're a real warrior now."

Not finding this amusing, Seon picked up his pack and stood up. It was a long walk to the forest, and they would not get there by dark. Still, it would be better to get as close as they could. Azoz followed without a word, even though he did have his characteristic smirk. Seon whistled, since Alix was nowhere near that he could see. She came whizzing down at his call and landed on his outstretched elbow.

"Hi, girl," Seon said, gently stroking her feathers. "Are you hurt at all?"

From the way she felt under his hand, it did not seem as if she was injured. He did sense some fatigue, but she appeared to be mostly rested and had satiated herself well on the insects she had caught. Seon was relieved. He hated to think that he might have brought her to harm.

"Is she okay?" Azoz asked.

"Yes," Seon said. "She will be. She's tired, like both of us."

Azoz just nodded at that, and the two of them continued on in silence. Seon wasn't interested in reasons or excuses from Azoz. As far as he was concerned, Azoz had disappeared and Seon had done fine on his own. Most of the time he had, at least, until he almost got squished by the giant purple lizard monster.

Fortunately, the day was proving uneventful. The sky was overcast, but it was no longer as cold as it had been. Rain sprinkled down on them from time to time, but Azoz ignored it and Seon did as well. The hats provided with their gear kept rain and sleet out of their eyes. The closer they got to the forest, the warmer the weather became. Even the rain was getting warmer.

"Do you know where we're going?" Seon asked, after they stopped walking to settle down for the night.

"No," Azoz said. "But you do."

"What makes you say that?" Seon wanted to scoff, but tried to keep his voice neutral.

"You're the one with the visions," Azoz said, "The one communicating with her."

"Yes, I am," Seon said. "And I do know where she is. You wouldn't be able to find her without me."

"Right," Azoz said. "That's why you're here."

It was difficult not to reply by asking why they'd left him, but Seon resisted. After all, he was tired of them playing games with him. Neither of them wanted to tell him anything. They gave him just enough information, and just enough training, to be their guide. It was frustrating but there was nothing he could do about it and Seon tried not to find it demeaning. He was here, and in his mind he was doing well considering his background. He had learned a lot about himself.

"I'm doing this on my terms," Seon said.

"What's that supposed to mean?" Azoz asked.

He didn't sound surprised. Maybe he did sound a little curious. Seon doubted he was interested.

"You can't just leave me whenever you feel like it, or tell me what to do," Seon said. "We are equals, or nothing. I will just go off on my own. Corin's not coming back?"

Azoz looked like he was going to say something, but he didn't. Seon wondered if he even knew the answer to that question. It was more of a relief to Seon not having Corin there, other than wondering when he was going to show up and want to take charge. Seon liked things better without him glaring and ordering all the time.

"So we're on our own," Seon concluded. "It doesn't matter, because we don't need him. We've proven that we can do this. I've proven it."

With a grunt, Seon reached down and grabbed an armful of logs. Azoz nodded and began collecting kindling. The two worked in silence as they made camp. Seon had not had any time to gather fruits, herbs, or vegetables and their stores were getting low. He was going to have to be on the lookout for them in the morning. They would have to make what they had work for the time being.

The meal was silent. It wasn't really an uneasy silence, but Seon was also antsy about what was to come. So as he ate, he tried to decide how much to tell Azoz. If they got separated again, Azoz would need to know where to go. Seon didn't know the name of the village or where exactly the farm was, but he knew the general direction, and Azoz should too if they got separated or one of them was too injured to continue. Worse, Seon had almost died. He didn't want to take the information to death with him when he could have passed it on.

"I know where she is," Seon said. "Not exactly, but close enough. I can find her. I reached out when she was ... communicating, and I was able to figure out where she is."

"That's major," Azoz said with a nod. "How'd you do it?"

"I don't know exactly," Seon admitted. "She was talking to me, you know, without talking. I can't see her face or hear actual words, which is frustrating. I know that she is on the edge of this forest though, which is why I have been heading toward it. There is a farm, on the outskirts of a village. I don't know the name of the village of course. I do not speak any of these languages."

"That doesn't matter," Azoz said. "You and Emili can communicate."

"We can," Seon agreed, "at a distance anyway. What happens when we are close to each other?"

"Why would it be any different?" Azoz asked.

Seon had not really considered why, but it was something that made him nervous. He had built Emili up in his mind. She was the person he had dreamed about for months. It wasn't a romantic connection, exactly. Maybe it was. He wasn't sure. He just knew that he longed for her, and longed to see her in person. He wanted to see what she looked like.

It was Azoz he wasn't sure about. Azoz seemed eager to meet Emili as well, and Seon wondered what their history was. He didn't ask about it because he wasn't sure he wanted to know. Azoz was enough of an enigma but if he didn't know where Emili was, then he couldn't have known her before. At least Seon didn't think it was possible. He tried not to think of it as jealousy, but maybe that's what it was, in a way.

He wanted Emili for himself.

Chapter 16

The next day dawned to drizzle. Seon and Azoz were both grumpy. At least Seon assumed Azoz was grumpy, because he barely said a word as they broke camp and set off toward the forest. Seon definitely felt he was justified in a case of the grumps. Their gear protected them from the worst of the moisture, but it was still dreary and the cloud cover made the day darker than usual. Alix didn't even make a shadow as she flew overhead.

"How much further do you think it is?" Seon asked.

"You're the one with the directions," Azoz said.

"Not exactly," Seon mumbled.

It was true that while he knew the general direction they were going, it was not as if he knew exactly where to go. That was a source of endless frustration for him. The night before, he had reached out with his senses, but had gotten nothing. It was as if the closer he came, the more closed off he was to her. Maybe he was trying too hard. For whatever reason, Emili was not calling him, and she was not responding either.

It had always been a lopsided relationship. In the beginning, he had never been able to call out to her and actually get a response. As he came to understand how it worked, and especially after Corin began training him in meditation, he had begun to call her and have her answer. More often than not, she called him. It was always like that. He wanted to be able to call her reliably.

"Realistically, we are almost to the forest, which means we are nearly to Silvax," Azoz said. "We can go into the village, or skirt the village and look for the farm. You said it is near a stream or brook and a lake. The lake is probably Lac Patet. We can just head off toward the lake and then look for a farm nearby. I am sure there is more than one, but from your description, it's probably somewhere between the lake and the village."

"I think we should skip the village," Seon said. "I look like a foreigner and I don't speak the language."

Azoz nodded. "In this part of the country, it is better not to stand out. Actually, I do too. It's better for both of us to blend in, hide in the woods, and try to make contact."

Considering this response, Seon thought about why Azoz might stand out. White-green hair and pale yellow skin must not be the norm around here. He thought back to the highwaymen and realized he had barely even noticed what they looked like, other than the unusual skin tones. He hadn't paid attention to their clothing much but he knew he didn't understand them and Azoz did. Then again, Azoz seemed to speak a few languages here.

"Let's just get as far as we can today," Seon said. "We need to look for food though."

With the weird first-to-forehead gesture that Seon had determined was a salute, Azoz walked off, presumably to hunt. Seon had noticed that he was also skilled in finding herbs, but his larger role was in hunting since Seon still refused to do so and they only had the meat Alix provided. This was not that big of a deal since Seon rarely ate meat, but he had eaten some when Azoz practically forced it on him and their stores were low.

Luckily, Seon was able to find a short scrubby bush that had tart, but edible berries that were lime green and looked and tasted like a sort of candy. Seon didn't bother drying them since there weren't very many and they were so small that they would shrink to nearly nothing. He had better luck looking for tubers, finding and pulling up a dozen of something yam-like. There were so many that if he hadn't had a magical storage sack he wouldn't have taken them all. They would be good in stews or mashed, and he found some herbs nearby to season them.

Before long, they stopped for a meal and Azoz roasted a small fowl he had caught. Seon wanted no part of that, but he roasted a few of the yams and some other vegetables, and they had the berries for dessert. It was a feast, and they had their fill. Alix came down and helped herself to some of the berries and yams, as well as some dried fish Seon had saved for her. There was little conversation, but it seemed more satisfied than grumpy for now.

"How much further do you think it is?" Seon asked Azoz after they had eaten.

The tree cover was getting thicker, even though they were not yet in the actual forest. The weather was not as cool as on the tundra, but neither was it hospitable. At least the rain seemed to have stopped for now. There were small flying insects taking a run at them as they ate, and Seon swatted them away every once in a while but mostly ignored them because they were so tiny he could barely see them and they didn't seem to bite. It was definitely getting closer to a forest landscape. He could sense the humming of active life.

In the distance, there was also more sentient life. Humans were nearby, but not that close. There were not that many of them. During the whole journey, Seon had almost never been close to humans. When he had been, he had steered clear. He wondered what it would be like when he was actually in a town or village, and especially a city like where he used to live. He was learning to close himself off to the sounds and feelings of animals. When there were so many more people, he was going to need to increase the process of blocking others out.

Seon got comfortable and let himself fall into a meditative trance, reaching out to feel the life forces of those around him.

He started with the tiny insects, and then the larger bushes, plants and trees, and the animals going about their business in the forest beyond. Even farther, there were people. He was careful not to touch them, in case one of them reached back for him. Emili was not answering, but Seon was not particularly searching for her. He was searching for something different this time, something elusive that he could feel at the edge of his consciousness. It was something he had felt the night before, but had been unable to identify or name.

Almost in a trance, Seon stood up and followed the silent call. He was remotely aware that he was moving, but not where or why. He knew that he had to move in the direction of the call. His eyes were barely open, but he felt certain that he would not trip. He could continue in that way indefinitely, until he found it, even though he was not consciously aware of what 'it' might be.

As if he were sleepwalking, Seon continued in this vein. He felt a buzzing in his hands, similar to the strongest sensation he felt when he was healing someone or something, so he decided to continue toward the buzzing. It reminded him of a game he used to play with his older brother, where they would yell out "you're hot," or "you're cold" when approaching some object the other had hidden. Seon was playing with the forest, looking for some powerful hidden object. It wasn't until he was almost on it that he realized what it could be.

"Oh," Seon said, out loud.

In his walk, he had gone deeper and deeper into the forest and came upon a stream. The water was running faster than he would have expected, probably because of the recent rain. It had uncovered the stones on the bottom of the stream. There were stones of different colors, but one stood out. It was a deep purple color. Seon kneeled down on the bank of the stream and reached into the water, pulling out the crystal that had been calling to him as surely as if it had been using words.

He picked it up and stared at it. Azoz had been right. He did belong to the Clan Amethyst. This was the right color and looked like an amethyst. It was not quite the same as the one Azoz had. It was slightly larger and not the same shape, but it was definitely the same stone.

"Wow," Seon said.

He gently rubbed the remnants of sand from the streambed off the stone, and then dried it off with his sleeve. Somehow, he felt in tune with the stone already. It should not be too much of a surprise, it had called to him, after all. He felt numb, staring at it.

"The storm charged it," Azoz said from behind him.

Seon started. He hadn't heard Azoz come up behind him. He nodded. He could feel the energy buzzing in the crystal. It seemed almost alive. The one Azoz had never called to him this way.

"You continue to surprise me," Azoz said, clapping Seon on the back soundly. "You must be more powerful than I thought."

Seon looked thoughtfully at the crystal, but shrugged. Azoz had never really explained the process to him other than saying the crystals were usually inherited through families or from the person you were apprenticed to. Seon was happy to have this one though. There was trouble ahead. He could feel it.

"Should we follow this in?" Seon asked, changing the subject. He gestured toward the creek.

Azoz nodded. Seon could tell he was just as relieved that they were finally in the forest. Their mission objective was in sight, or at least closer. Emili was somewhere on the other side of this stream, and she had a crystal like this one.

Seon held up the stone.

"This should help me find Emili," he said, wishing he could be more confident.

"Maybe," Azoz agreed. "She has one. You have to learn to use it. It's not in tune with you completely yet. Enough that you found it. It called you. That's a start." He paused. "That's really rare.'

As far as Seon was concerned, he was tired of hearing how rare he was. He just wanted to find Emili. They were so close now. He was getting impatient, or having a premonition of danger. He wasn't sure what it was.

"You should try to contact her again after you have worn it for a while," Azoz said. "I will make you an amulet with it."

Seon agreed. He was curious to see what Azoz would come up with, and looked back now and then as Azoz braided him a necklace and pouch out of some of the leather cord he carried around. At least it was more useful than whittling. When they stopped for a break and meal, he looked in on the progress and saw that there was an intricate pattern to the braids. Although Seon could not make sense of it, he wondered what it meant.

"It's to keep you safe," Azoz explained, taking it back from Seon and continuing on with his work.

"Right," Seon said, although he was not quite sure how that was supposed to work.

They each ate in silence, nibbling on dried fruit and, in Azoz's case, meat. Seon was tired and did not feel like making conversation, and Azoz seemed to be concentrating on his braiding and whatever spells he was weaving into the talisman. He was grateful for it, but also more than a little wary at the same time. He had yet to fully trust Azoz. He found himself wondering if Azoz could track him with this somehow.

I'm being paranoid.

Seon leaned back against a moss-covered stone that seemed to almost make a pillow. He sent a gentle suggestion to the tiny ants and bugs to leave him alone, and they scattered. Insects were a way of life in the forest, but Seon wanted to concentrate without interruption, and they tickled.

Emili. ... Emili, are you there?

As he called, he held the amethyst close in his hand. He could feel its warmth, and it seemed to buzz with life again, as if it was calling too. Since he did not yet understand how things worked, he realized that it might be doing just that, and tried to add his own power to the stone's.

He felt a response. It wasn't in words or emotions. As usual, it was more of a pull, grasping out for him as he grasped out for it.

Emili it's me! We are close. Are you alright? Do you need help? Is there danger?

It was a question that Seon had considered from all angles. Until he came closer, it had been academic and although they had discussed it early on, Seon was certain that he had been left out of most of the important dialogue.

At first, there was no response. He did not expect words, but he had expected something. Then, he felt something that he could only describe as amusement. He wasn't sure whether that was in response to his question or the idea that he was suggesting he would rescue her. He neither meant that he was afraid or that he was coming to the rescue. He had never had any indication that she was afraid. He didn't think that she was being held prisoner. It was more like she was waiting. And he had no idea why.

That was one of the many questions he was planning to ask her, when he finally was in a position to get some answers. In the meantime, he was just happy to be able to communicate more freely, as the crystal seemed to be able to facilitate more open communication. It wasn't words or images. It was more like telepathy. The concept seemed to amuse Emili.

I'm glad you find me so amusing. Emili, this is serious. I need to know what I'm getting into. What we're getting into. You might not be in danger, but we are. They are coming for us. There's ... someone ... with me. Kind of a friend.

Since he was not sure how to explain Azoz's presence and he wasn't sure if Emili knew that Azoz was with him, he tried to leave it at that. He didn't get any kind of reaction, and at first he wasn't even sure if she was there. Then there was a sensation that felt sort of like a question.

Who is he? Why is he here? Hmm. Well ... he brought me here. I guess he sort of showed me the way, for a little bit. And then I showed him.

It was kind of hard to explain. Azoz and Corin had shown Seon the portal, or at least they had taken him through it. He didn't think he ever would have gotten this far without them. But they definitely would never have found Emili without Seon. It was the reason they had brought him. It wasn't necessarily a good thing, though, his bringing Azoz here. He wasn't sure of their motives. They wanted to find her, but they hadn't told him why. They told him very little. In exchange, he trusted them very little.

Yet here he was, a stone's throw from Emili, and Azoz was still with him. If it came to a fight, he was probably better off with Azoz than on his own. Unfortunately, it would depend on who he was fighting. He couldn't fight Azoz. He still didn't know what side Azoz was on.

And what about Seon. Whose side was he on?

On the other side of their telepathic bond, he knew Emili was asking him that same thing.

Chapter 17

"The village is here," Azoz drew a map with a stick. "More than likely there are several farms along the banks of the river and the creek. You will be able to identify which one it is. The problem might be that we are not the only ones looking."

"How would the Umbra know where to look?" Seon asked the question that had been bothering him.

"We can't discount the possibility that they are tracking us," Azoz said. "Or, they might be watching her."

These ideas made Seon's insides go cold. He hated to think that the Shadow Men might find Emili before they did, or that they might find Seon and Azoz before they found Emili. The last few days had been so terrifying and busy that he had almost forgotten about them. It was easy to get caught up in the moment and forget the bigger picture when you were fighting for your life.

"How?" Seon asked, whispering even though doing so was probably completely ridiculous. " How are they tracking us?"

He expected Azoz to give him the 'you're an idiot look' he often got, but instead Azoz just shrugged. "It could be any number of ways. Probably from our tracks or from the air."

"The air?"

"They might be tracking us through our scent. They know who I am now, and they found me once before," Azoz looked thoughtful. "We have to get there as soon as possible. It's not long now."

"No," Seon said, remembering when Azoz had been attacked back in the city.

Seon could feel that they were closer. It might have been instinct, or the conversation with Emili, or maybe just nerves. He thought that the crystal he had now might have also had something to do with it. It was an awakening. Something was happening, and they were a part of it. There would soon be no stopping it.

"Is there anything we can do to counter it?" Seon asked.

"Without knowing how or if they are tracking us, not really," Azoz said. "I have taken precautions, of course."

"You have? I haven't. What precautions?" Seon asked.

"We clean our camp," Azoz said. "You have done the same. Of course our boots are spelled to not leave footprints or scents."

"That doesn't stop them from getting stuck in footprints," Seon noted grimly.

"Well no, there's always user error," Azoz said with a grin.

"What about Alix?" Seon asked. "They might know her?"

"Maybe," Azoz agreed. "She does stand out. Her colors are dull here. She has a particular scent, and if they know she is your familiar, they can track her too. She can take care of herself though."

That was one thing Seon had to agree with. Alix was definitely more of an asset than a liability. Besides her ability to hunt and fight, she was a companion he didn't feel he could do without. He had grown to rely on her as if she had always been there.

"What is your suggestion if we do come upon them?" Seon asked.

After a moment of giving that question some consideration, Azoz stood up. "Use our minds and keep our wits about us. You and I haven't sparred for a while, right?

"Right," Seon said with a sigh.

They spent the next few hours sparring and brushing Seon up on fighting against opponents who were bigger, stronger, and outnumbered him. They made several contingency plans based on what they'd learned from the highwaymen. Seon grimly accepted the scenarios and the instruction. He'd been angry at Azoz for killing the men when they didn't know the full extent of the threat they posed, but he was starting to understand better the choice Azoz had made. He still didn't have to like it, but after what Seon had been through with the giant lizard, the ants, the fire, and the elephant, he had to grudgingly see the wisdom in Azoz's move. Sometimes it was kill or be killed.

What Seon was pleasantly surprised to see was that he had managed to develop some muscle in a short period of time. Azoz smirked at him and said that eating magical herbs tended to have that effect. That made Seon nervous, but he would take what he could get right now. In the back of his mind, he worried about the consequences. Getting too many muscles too fast did not seem like a good idea, even if he had earned some of them.

Muscle wasn't everything though, Seon noted as Azoz flattened him for the dozenth time. Muscle memory and technique were also important, as well as skill. Azoz had it all over him in those respects. They had been working on this one technique for bringing down a stronger opponent for over an hour, and Seon was exhausted. He wasn't getting it, and it was frustrating to him. Azoz wasn't letting up either. He just kept coming at Seon, methodically knocking him down as if this were as easy for him as a stroll through a summer picnic.

"Let up already," Seon said, not standing from the last time he had been knocked down. "I'm tired and I'm not getting it."

"Is that what you're going to say to your enemy?" Azoz said, looming over Seon and giving him a mighty kick in the ribs to emphasize the point. "I'm too tired, come back later!"

Seon growled, and tried to kick back up at Azoz, who was too fast. He knew what Azoz was doing. Unfortunately, it was working. He was angry enough with Azoz to be riled despite being tired, but he was still tired, and still slower than Azoz. Rolling around on the dirt floor of the forest wasn't going to help him get back at Azoz any faster. Instead, he lay where he was and focused all of his efforts on the roots at Azoz's feet, trying to get Azoz to think they were someplace else.

Seon jumped to his feet and ran at Azoz, clumsily but at least in the right direction. As he ran, he projected an image of the forest floor into the other's mind—without the roots. When he charged. Azoz ran backwards, surprised by the sudden momentum and energy that Seon seemed to have. Seon was surprised too. He must be pulling it from somewhere, but at the moment, he didn't take the time to analyze the situation and dissect where he was getting it from. He just charged at Azoz while he fell backward over roots he did not see, and then Seon landed on top of him.

"What in Plutes did you just do?" Azoz demanded, shaking his head in pain and confusion as he hit a particularly large tree root.

"I used my mind and kept my wits about me," Seon said.

"Right," Azoz said with a grimace, pushing Seon off of him not at all gently. "I guess you did. You made me think the root wasn't there?"

Seon nodded. He could not help but be pleased with himself for finally getting one over on Azoz. He had also learned a trick that would be useful. Seon could tell Azoz was grudgingly respectful as he stood up and brushed moss and sticks away from his clothes.

"This is good," he said. "We can work with this."

It was Seon's turn to grin, feeling as if he had finally done something right. They spent the rest of the afternoon perfecting the technique, or at least making sure that Seon was better at it. It took a lot more out of him than just brute force. Any mental magic did. In the end, Seon was glad to have another tool in his arsenal.

That night, Seon slept more deeply than usual. He dreamed of running through the fields by Emili's farm in the carefree manner that he had not done for months. The dream ended suddenly with a feeling of dread. He wasn't sure whether he had cut it short or if she had.

Seon sat up and realized he was in a cold sweat. He could not shake the feeling that they were in danger. Looking around, he saw that Azoz was nowhere near, even though it seemed to be the middle of the night based on the darkness and the moon. That alone was not cause for concern, except for the feeling that Seon had.

Getting up quietly, Seon put his pack on and walked quietly to the edge of their camp. They had made sure that everything was packed before they fell asleep, using their sacks as pillows. This close to civilization, it was best not to take any chances with a full camp or a fire. Seon fully saw the wisdom of that move now. He had no way to track Azoz.

Seon crept over to a tree and pulled his crystal out of the protective leather tear-drop shaped amulet around his neck. Azoz had only finished it that evening, and as Seon's fingers grazed the braids, he was relieved by that fact. He idly wondered if somehow having this crystal would make it easier to find Azoz, as he could sense Emili. He had never been able to do that before, but then, he had never tried.

Now did not seem like the best time or place to try that way, however. It was dark, and there might be danger. So instead, Seon used the time to slink through the trees as quietly and quickly as he could. He knew the general direction he should head in order to avoid the town while still going toward where he thought Emili might be. If Azoz had spotted danger and gone after it, the best thing Seon could do was head toward their final destination and hope Seon found him.

Since the danger was still unclear, Seon reached into his sheathe and retrieved his knife and carried it in his hand. He reached out with his sensory awareness while also attempting to read the general impressions of the animals in the forest. He did not pick up any more than the sleepy alertness that was usually found at this time of night. Some of the animals were hunting and some were trying to avoid being hunted, while others were lurking. There was no sign of Azoz or anything else sentient, at least not within the short sphere he'd cast out.

It was not much further, he knew, before the forest became less dense and there were inhabited areas. There was a village and some farms. That must be where Azoz had gone, but the question was why. It would not be the first time Seon had been abandoned by one or both of them and neither of them had ever given him an explanation, but there seemed to be something more sinister at play here. Seon knew that Azoz had not been abducted. It made no sense for anyone to take Azoz and not him. That meant that Azoz had gone on his own, and then something had happened.

Walking through the woods in the dark, Seon was wishing he had gotten more lessons on tracking. Corin had taught him a few cursory skills, and Azoz had added to the lessons when they had been together on their travels, but his instruction was really quite lacking. Especially given the fact that there were no footprints to go by and Azoz was an expert at not leaving signs unless he wanted to, Seon was at a loss unless he wanted to sit down and meditate in the middle of the forest, leaving himself vulnerable.

At an impasse, Seon stopped and closed his eyes briefly, sending a call to Alix with his mind as quickly as he could. She came, wafting through the trees. Clearly she had not been that far away. He sent her a mental image to watch his back, and then nestled into the trunk of a tree and closed himself off in a deep meditation, focusing on his crystal and trying to reach out to Azoz. He had never done this before, and the feeling of searching was different than with Emili. For several minutes there was no response.

Then, suddenly, he felt a burst of pain.

He had made the connection with Azoz, and it had confirmed his worst fear. Azoz was in trouble.

Seon reached out again, and tried to concentrate on the connection to find Azoz. He tried to ask where he was, what was happening, and what he could do. Seon wanted to get up and run toward the sense of where Azoz was, but at the same time he didn't want to break the connection. It seemed wiser to be calm and find as much information as possible first.

Where are you? What happened? What can I do?

At first, there was no reply. Then Seon got a clear response, a reply that came through almost a shockingly clear as a picture on a video screen.

Run!

Chapter 18

"Take me to him," Seon said.

He held the crystal out in front of him, imploring it to do his bidding. Of course, it was doing no such thing. The crystal might as well have been a useless rock for all the good it did, sitting listlessly in his hand. Seon squeezed it, closing his eyes and willing it into action. It was no use. Nothing happened.

The point seemed made. Azoz was in trouble, or at least in danger and in pain. Seon was not going to be able to help him. He was once again on his own. Seon felt useless and frustrated. Whereas before, he had been annoyed at Azoz for leaving him high and dry to fend for himself, now he did not know how to feel about his situation. He wasn't sure this time what the circumstances were behind Azoz's leaving Seon and how he had ended up where he was, and he was inclined to cut him more slack, maybe because he knew that Azoz was in some kind of situation and he needed Seon.

Seon wasn't sure why he felt the need to save Azoz. Maybe it was because Azoz had rescued him, and he wanted to return to favor. It could just be that he felt that it was bad form to leave someone behind if you knew that he was in a situation.

If the crystal somehow led him to Azoz passively, Seon wanted to be prepared. So he closed his eyes, centered himself, sent a reminder to Alix to watch his back, and headed off in the direction his instincts told him to go. The sun was starting to rise in that he could see the very beginnings of daybreak in the distance, but it would be awhile before it was light enough to call day.

As quickly as he could without sacrificing stealth, Seon continued through the forest. He had been taught how to move through the forest without making a sound. The boots helped, of course. They made him light on his feet and they didn't leave a mark. He was careful also to not to leave other indications of his presence, never brushing against the trees or knocking over a stone on the forest floor.

It seemed to take days, when in reality Seon knew the journey was only hours. By the time the sun had fully arisen, he did not feel like he was any closer to the village or to the farm. He planned to skirt the village and the forest's edge when he got that far. Ultimately, he was not sure what he would find there, and it was the not knowing that scared him the most. He had not expected to be on his own at this point, since yesterday Azoz had been with him. Today he was, and he would have to make the most of it.

Alix swooped down from overhead and landed on his shoulder, startling Seon. He looked around, half-spinning in a circle to see what might have startled her. While her presence close by was comforting, he was also wary. She usually didn't land without him calling her. If there was some other danger, she normally stayed overhead where she was in a better position to defend both herself and him. By landing on him now, she seemed to be signaling the danger came from an unknown source.

With a great deal of care, Seon moved forward into a clearing. These could be found throughout the forest, natural clearings where trees had fallen, brooks or streams crossed, or other natural gaps in the trees opened the landscape. Every time Seon came to one, he moved extra carefully. Less cover meant he was not as able to move quickly. While something might have dropped down on him from above, he relied more on Alix to be on the lookout for those threats. She seemed to believe that there was no threat there, at least now. A threat might be somewhere ahead, though, and Seon was cautious.

At this point, Seon saw nothing in the clearing but trees. There were a few fallen trees, just like at other points in the forest. The logs lay about, criss-crossed along the forest floor. There were leaves, sticks, and small bushes just like everywhere else. In short, there was nothing out of the ordinary. Seon was beginning to think that he and the hawk both had overactive imaginations. Then he saw it.

Off to the edge of the clearing was what Seon had at first thought was just another pile of logs covered in moss. It wasn't though. When he looked deeply enough, he could see two eyes under the moss. It wasn't moss at all. Sitting on the log at the edge of the clearing, was Emili.

Are you alright?

It seemed like a dumb question as soon as he asked it. Of course he did not ask it out loud, with words. He spoke with his mind, to her mind, just as he always did. He also did not move. Emili was so well camouflaged in her moss-cored cloak that standing there, in the breaking down, he could almost convince himself that he was imagining her. He had dreamed of seeing her for months, and there she was, real for the first time, still not moving. Still not talking. Not even blinking. Leave it to Seon to ask a stupid question.

Of course I'm alright! It took you long enough to get here. I've been waiting for ages.

Seon smiled at Emili's response. *Yeah, sorry. I got a little held up. You could have given us better directions.*

Emili grinned, and finally stood. She tossed back the hood of her cloak, and rivulets of early sun fell on the tresses of her hair.

Seon saw that the color was almost the same as the hood, closer to tree bark than moss, but somewhere in between. Not quite as green as Azoz's, dark while his was electric green, hers was earthy. Seon thought it was gorgeous. It accented violet colored eyes that were almost pink and a color he had never seen at home. Her skin was the color of tree-bark, rich but calloused on her hands where she had obviously used them in hard work.

Us? Emili's expression also asked the question

Seon considered. *There was ... someone ... with me. A friend I guess. I am not sure what happened to him. He might be hurt.*

Hurt? How? Emili seemed frustrated.

Her concern was evident. Seon wished he had more information. The truth was he had almost forgotten that he was looking for Azoz in the excitement of having found Emili. Now he was not sure what to do. If it were not for the possibility that Azoz was hurt or in danger, he would not have looked for him at all or even told Emili about him. He still did not trust Azoz or Corin fully. Now he felt like telling her was endangering her.

Maybe it's better that I don't ... Seon found himself unable to finish the sentence.

That you don't what? Tell me about your friend? Emili's eyes snapped passionately, but anger or worry Seon could not tell.

I don't want to endanger you too, if he is in danger. Seon tried to make her see that he was earnest.

Is that your decision to make? Emili's eyes bore into him.

It wasn't.

Seon nodded. Not being able to speak in words was both freeing and frustrating at the same time. There was an emotional vulnerability about it, as if he was unable to hide the truth of his feelings. He wasn't sure if we wanted to. He had always been more open than not with Emili.

You don't trust him. Do you trust me?

I trust you.

He could not help but trust her. She was inside his head, and while he never really felt that he was inside hers, he trusted her. He wondered why she would ask.

You have been calling to me. Why?

I should think that would be obvious. Because you can hear me.

There was no haughtiness to her reply. Her tone had the same light teasing that she always seemed to use with him. Her answer did make sense.

Fair enough. Why? Why can I hear you?

We are linked, you and I. Even before you found your crystal.

He was surprised to hear her say that. It was still in his hand though, and he ran his thumb over the smooth surface. She might have seen it, after all.

You have one too?

She nodded, and then reached inside a pouch around her neck to withdraw a small, dagger-shaped crystal of a hue similar to his own. The pinkish-purple caught the light and he could see that it was almost clear. It was beautiful, small and strong. It called to him, or maybe to his own crystal.

Wow.

Yes.

She reached out, and when the two crystals touched, there was a mild flash of rose-colored light. Seon felt a shock of electricity, like when he had walked across a carpeted floor back home without picking up his feet. He balked, almost dropping his crystal. They seemed magnetized together.

What happened?

Mine was charged. So was yours. They shared a charge.

She smiled.

What does that mean?

We are connected. We can call each other now, through the crystals, over great distances, and easier than before.

Considering this, Seon realized that could be very helpful. After all, he had often contacted Emili only with great effort and it had never been this easy to talk to her before. He had never been standing as close. He wondered, though, what she wanted with him. She still hadn't said. She reminded him of Azoz that way.

Why? Why would we need to?

Because. You and I have things to do.

Like what. You haven't told me anything. You contacted me. You let me hear. You still have not told me why. You all seem to think that just because I can, I will.

Why wouldn't you?

Seon could tell she was amused.

Why would I?

Boys. All you ever want is adventure.

He couldn't tell if she was teasing him or not. Either way, Seon was not amused. He frowned at her.

Maybe I'm not like other boys. Maybe I'm not the adventuring type.

You're not? She looked him up and down, clearly looking at his clothing and the beat-up gear, the knife in his hand, and his overall appearance of having been in a fight or two over the last few days.

I was forced into this. I was basically kidnapped. They made me come.

You didn't want to? Why not?

Seon thought about that. Now that he was here, he was glad for the fact that he had come. He had been forced. This was not his fight before, but it was now.

It doesn't matter. I'm here now. I am Clan Amethyst now because I have been chosen by Clan Amethyst. I may not understand your ways and your language, but I am learning.

Emili nodded. *You can learn, if you want to.*

It might be nice to understand the language. Can you speak out loud?

Of course. She laughed again, a musical laugh. *But you do not speak my language and I do not speak yours.*

Figures. Seon shrugged. *We are going to have to learn, one or the other.*

They walked side by side along the forest as the sun rose. She made him feel relaxed for the first time in days. He knew that was a strange thing. This was the person who had dragged him away from his safe, normal home, almost literally from his bed. He should resent her for it.

Somehow, she did not make him feel used or less than she was, despite his first reaction. Seon just never had been able to talk to girls, especially Emili. It wasn't that he had fallen for her, despite Azoz's teasing to that effect. It was just that the situation was so strange and confusing. Seon barely felt comfortable with anyone, let alone her, even though she talked to him in his dreams and inside his own head.

What's really going on? Why did you call me?

After they had walked for a bit, Seon asked the question he felt he deserved an answer to. He did not want cryptic hints about wars between those who wanted magic and those who didn't, he just wanted to know why he was there. It was time someone told him. If he was so important to what happened, he needed to know what to do.

I was lonely. I found you, so far away, and I found I could talk to you. The more I did, the more I wanted to.

It's not that simple.

Seon may not know all the inns and outs of this world, but he knew nothing was that easy. There was more to it that she wasn't telling him, and he wanted to know why. He stopped walking, determined not to go farther until he had the answer.

Emili smiled. *Why must you know every drop of water before it falls?*

Not every drop, but I like to know when there's going to be a storm before I step out in it, yeah.

She laughed, and Seon could not get enough of that laugh. It was like a birdsong, as if it came from the forest itself. Emili was free and easy but Seon had seen her up close and now that he had, he could tell that she was as muscular as she was lithe. He knew that she could take care of herself in a fight.

We did not come here to rescue you, did we?

To rescue me?

She seemed more amused than offended by that idea. Seon would have been offended in her place. He had never seen any girl who looked less in need of rescuing. She looked like she could wipe the forest floor with him.

I didn't think so. So I am here for some other reason. Because I belong here. Because this is my fight, apparently.

Seon pondered this, looking at the forest around him. This one looked so much more like the ones back home that he had barely noticed it since he had been in it. The trees were slightly greener than brown, and the plants were not the same shapes and colors as back home, but nothing was vividly different. Emili was the most unusual-looking thing here, and he knew girls and even boys who dyed their hair and wore make-up and contacts to change their natural coloring.

It is better for us to be together, now. Don't you think?

Us? Who is us?

The ones who will save the world.

Seon stared at Emili for a few moments, trying to wrap his head around how he would save the world. He assumed she meant her world, and not his. It was his world too now. The world he came from seemed like a distant memory.

Right. How do we do that exactly?

The bigger questions in his head might have been why the world needed saving and from whom, or perhaps why he needed to be the one to save it. The whole world-saving thing seemed like hyperbole though, so he decided to stick to the more practical question. Find the girl, save the world. He had found the girl. Now he needed to save the world.

You don't believe me.

It's not that I don't believe you. My ... friends ... also told me something similar. They said there was a war coming, between the magic users and the ones who believe that no one should have magic, or maybe no one should have magic but them. Is that what you're talking about?

Yes. That's them. The one who thinks that no one should have magic, he is brutal. He's dangerous, and he is after me. He's after you, probably. He might have your friend, the one who's missing.

That made sense to Seon. He had been worried that the Umbra had gotten Azoz somehow, and that Azoz might have sensed danger and gone looking for it, and that was the reason he was missing. He started, realizing what Emili had said.

He is after you, then. That is what I thought. They never really said, but I assumed so. The Umbra are looking for you? Why?

It's because of their leader. His name is Hadrian. He is powerful. He has many Gifts, not just one or two like most people. He is almost unstoppable. But me, I have more. Even more than him.

That is why he is looking for you? It was starting to make sense to Seon. If Emili was as powerful as she said, no wonder they were looking for her.

Partly.

Why does he want you? Just because you are powerful?

People fear what they do not understand. And what they cannot control.

He wants to control you? Seon wondered why anyone would fear Emili. She looked tough, but not frightening. Then again, he wasn't sure yet what she could do.

Emil looked at Seon with an unreadable expression on her face. It was akin to sadness. She gestured, and a small piece of bark flew across the forest floor into her hand. Seon jumped back, not expecting it.

See this? She put it into his hand. It was an ordinary piece of bark, light and porous. Seon nodded. Emili took it back from him. *Watch.*

She took the piece of bark and held it in an outstretched hand, and then closed her fingers over it, and squeezed. She opened her hand, and showed him. It had blackened to a crisp, like charcoal. She squeezed again, and then opened her hand. This time, it was clear and hard, like a diamond. She handed it to him. It was cool to his touch.

Wow. Impressive.

She gave him a sad smile.

It's just an example. I can do lots of things. I find new things all the time. I am good in a fight.

I'll bet.

Right. I can see why.

So that's one reason Hadrian wants me. Partly to prevent others from getting me, and partly to get me on his side.

Hadrian? Seon repeated the name as a question.

The leader of the Umbra. My brother.

Chapter 20

Hadrian is your brother?

Seon tried to let that sink in. He had never heard anything good about Hadrian, even though he had never known the man's name until now. Most of the information he knew about him was from comments made from Azoz, and information Corin had deemed necessary for him to have, which was frustratingly less than Seon had felt he should have.

I have never met him, of course. Emili added. *He is also much older than me.*

Seon nodded. He was not sure how old Emili was, but she was near his age. If Hadrian had built himself an evil empire and had henchmen running around trying to kidnap people, he had to be older than she was. One way or another, he seemed to be the type of person Seon wanted to avoid.

What does he want? Other than to prevent the spread of magic users?

What do people like him always want? Emili's eyes snapped with an anger Seon had not seen yet in her. *He wants to control people. He wants to make the world the way* he *thinks it should be. People like him always think they know best. They think that as long as they are doing it for what they feel are the right reasons, they can do anything they want.*

What are the reasons?

Not having been around magic long, Seon did not completely understand the arguments for and against it. He did see why people could fear those who were different, and he did understand fearing people who were magical. Magic was power, and people feared the powerful. People normally feared what they did not understand. When people did not understand magic, and feared it, Seon could see the trouble.

The main reason is that they don't think that everyone should use magic. They don't think most people are responsible enough. Magic users should be carefully regulated and put in prison if they misuse their magic.

That's terrible. Seon was horrified at the idea of being regulated for having magic, especially since he barely knew how to use it. He could easily see making a mistake that put him in prison. The fire sprang to mind. *We can't let that happen.*

Here, no one knows I am a magic user. I am hiding on a farm. A kind couple took me in, about a year and a half ago I started to get ... premonitions of danger. Then I started searching for others, and I found you. Emili looked at him soulfully.

Fat lot of good I turned out to be. Seon apologized.

Well, it helped, just to have someone to talk to. Even if we really could not talk. Just having you there made me feel less alone.

Seon understood. He had often felt the same way. Back home, no one had really understood him and he had likewise not understood them, without realizing why until he had met Azoz and Corin and found out the truth about himself. They might have dragged him here against his will, but he did feel more at home now, and more comfortable with himself.

What is the trouble? The danger that you felt coming? Your brother?

Emili did not answer right away. Seon was not sure if it was because she was thinking about her response, or trying to decide whether or not to respond. Finally, she nodded.

Partly. The danger does not come only from him. Some people agree with him. They will join with him, to avoid a fight or because it seems to make sense.

Yes, I know. Seon agreed. *I have seen that too. In my world, that has happened.*

People have to decide between what is easy and what seems safe. Emili was thoughtful. *They will give away freedoms for what seems to be security. They will make a deal with a monster that smiles sweetly.*

That's your brother? The smiling monster? Seon found the image disturbing.

Definitely.

Do you think they have Azoz? My friend. The Shadow Men might have him. He was gone when I woke up last night. I was looking for him when I found you. Seon felt guilty about having been distracted, remembering that he had been worried something had happened to Azoz and had started looking for him.

It's possible. I have not seen anyone, and I am careful. I knew you were nearby, and felt you reach out to me, so I came here to wait. It would not be good for you to come to the farm looking for me.

Because the family you live with do not know?

They do not know what I am. Emili looked as if it pained her to say this. *It is safer for them not to know.*

What if they come looking for you? The Shadow Men? What if I have led them right to that family? Seon hoped his voice, or at least what substituted for it inside her head, did not betray the panic that he felt.

He would not be able to live with himself if she had protected these people for a year and then he brought destruction upon them by stupidly coming too close. Their plan, his and Azoz's, had been reckless, he realized. They were all in danger.

I worry about that. Emili looked down, as if meeting his eyes was too painful. *Every day I have to decide, should I stay or should I go?*

Where would you go? On that note, Seon was not sure where he was going to go. *Do you have other family, besides the maniacal brother I mean?*

Emili shook her head. *None alive, except my Clan. You are my Clan.* She gestured to his crystal.

Right. Seon sighed. He figured if the answer had been 'yes', she would not be hiding with a farmer who didn't know who she really was. Especially with a brother like that.

Okay. So we do not go back there? Do we?

No. Emili said this firmly, neither sadly nor hesitantly. *We can try to find your friend though. Do you have an idea where he might have gone? What happened to him?*

Unfortunately, I think it's that way. Seon gestured in the direction he had been heading, which he knew was in the direction of the village and Emili's farm.

I guess we go find him then. She started in that direction.

Do you think he went there, looking for you? We could be leading them directly to the farm. Seon bit his lip. *It could be a trap.*

Do you have any better ideas? Her violet-pink eyes snapped in annoyance, and Seon had to admit she had a point.

No, I guess not. I could try to look for him again.

What are you waiting for then? It was a question, but it sounded more like a command.

Seon nodded, and walked over to a nearby tree. Alix flew off his arm and surprised Seon by landing on Emili's shoulder. She stroked the bird's feathers delicately and spoke soothingly, out loud, in a language Seon did not recognize. It was beautiful and musical, and it was the first time he had ever heard her speak out loud. Seon was mesmerized.

When Seon did not immediately get to work, Emili gave him a look that was a cross between annoyed and amused. Recognizing it for what it was, he smirked at her and settled back against the tree and got to work. Relaxing into a meditative posture, he found his center as quickly as possible given the distraction of his mind, and then reached out for Azoz.

Azoz ... where are you? Are you hurt?

Nothing. Seon continued the call for a few minutes, and then just searched, listening and looking for the presence he had come to associate with Azoz. Once he focused enough to find it, he realized that Azoz was there, but he was dampened, as if he was asleep or drugged. Seon thought that was a bad sign either way. Azoz would not choose either one on his own.

As soon as Seon realized that he had found Azoz, he tried to get a feel for the room around him, and farther out, to see where he was. There were no people near him, but there were people close. Seon tried to tell how many people were there, but for some reason it was hard for him to differentiate them. He thought maybe the distance was making it difficult, or his emotions were just getting in his way. Whatever the reason, he couldn't tell if there were three or six. There were definitely people around Azoz in what might have been rooms. He was being held prisoner. It had to be the Shadow Men.

Seon opened his eyes and looked around the forest. He had become disoriented, almost forgetting where he was. Emili was standing not far off, still stroking Alix as the bird perched on her shoulder.

I know where he is. He's been captured or kidnapped. There are a few men guarding him, but I could not get a fix on how many. I am still figuring that part out. What do I do?

You mean what do we *do?* Her eyes showed what she thought of his question.

It's not your fight. You don't even know him. You probably wouldn't like him. I don't like him. But I can't leave him there.

Exactly. Which is why we have to make a plan, and then go get him.

Seon couldn't deny her logic. The problem was that there were only two of them, and while Emili was tougher and much more powerful than he was, Seon still had no idea what to do. He looked at her pleadingly.

If the Umbra are here, and Azoz ran into them somehow and they took him, where might they take him? You know the area better than I do. Is this a trap to lure me? To lure you? As he said this, Seon realized it was likely both.

Of course. You know what to do with a trap.

What? Seon sympathized with animals. He did not like traps.

Spring the trap.

Again, he could not fault the logic.

Right. Let's spring the trap.

Emili grinned, and Alix took off into the air. Seon smiled back at Emili, feeling lighter than before, and they walked through the forest more or less side by side for the next few hours. By the time they reached the village, it was midday. Seon felt much more confident about approaching the village now that she was with him. Everything seemed possible now that she was with him.

Just as Seon had suspected, they did not approach the village directly. Instead, they skirted the edge of the forest and the village outskirts making sure to use the trees for as much cover as they provided. There were few people out even at what seemed like it would be a busy time of day.

Silvax. Emili gestured toward the village with a nod. *The people are frightened.*

Of what? It explained why there was no one outside the village. It was making Seon nervous. The place had an eerie feel.

I don't know. Emili looked unsettled. She must have felt what he felt, or he was feeling what she was feeling, and that was why he thought the village was eerie. It was not just the absence of people outside it. It was just too quiet. *There is something malevolent here.*

Always, or just now? Seon looked around. Nothing about the village seemed unusual, based on what he had seen in this place. There were stone buildings about two stories tall and houses with thatched roofs and wood shingles. It was old-fashioned looking, but not evil. *What's wrong with it?*

It's ... there's something here. Emili stopped, and closed her eyes. She seemed to be stretching out with her senses the way Seon did when he was trying to get the feel of a place. He thought maybe she could tell the energy of the town like he could from plants and animals and, to a certain extent, people. *And no, not always. I do not spend much time here though. It is safer not to.*

That made sense to Seon. If he was on the run, he wouldn't hang out where there were a lot of people. Silvax was a small village, but people might still travel through it. Emili would avoid attracting attention.

Where are we headed? Seon was still watching the village and Emili.

There's an abandoned mine on the outskirts of town. She opened her eyes as she answered him. *If they have him, that's where he is.*

How do you know? Seon didn't want to show doubt, but he was getting more nervous the closer they got.

That's where I'd go. She said simply.

Right.

Chapter 21

They continued through the woods on the outskirts of town. Seon could see the rooftops through the trees in the distance. They were just barely visible. Alix flew out of sight every once in a while and then returned just when Seon started to wonder where she was. The journey took much less time than it felt like to Seon, but his nerves were more on edge with every passing step.

When they came to a clearing, Emili stopped. They had been slowing down, so her stopping did not surprise Seon. Azoz had to be nearby. Seon reached out with his senses without closing his eyes, but he was careful about it. He didn't want to alert anyone with a Gift for sensing people.

Is he in there? She looked the question when she asked it.

Seon nodded. Since he was being careful, it was faint, but he could sense Azoz inside. They were too far away to see the entrance to the mine.

Your plan? Seon asked.

Emili was focused on the mountain. Seon wasn't sure what she was doing, and he wondered when she was going to let him in on it. As much as he liked Emili, it was starting to drain on him to be standing outside the lair of dangerous magic-wielding criminals with another powerful and possibly unstable magic-user when he himself barely knew how to use his own magic.

Emili? Seon asked again.

She sent a haughty look at him, and then nodded her head in the direction of the mine. Seon looked back toward it. At first, he did not know what he was looking at. Then he realized that a wisp of smoke was coming toward them.

What did you ...?

He didn't get to finish the question, because Emili was moving more quickly toward the smoke. She jumped up a tree in a move that he would never be able to replicate. He stared after her, realizing that she had just jumped straight up a distance that was twice her height, and then looked back toward the smoke. Distracted only for a moment, he moved off to the side of another tree and hid behind it.

Smoke was pouring out of the opening in the mountain now. Since they were closer, Seon could see that it was a large gap shored up with roughly-hewn wooden boards. He hadn't been watching it long when men began to come out of the doorway as well. There were two first, and then two more. They were wearing clothing similar to Seon's, but the leather tunics were darker, almost black, and even from the distance Seon could see they were practically shiny.

Another man came out of the mine, and this one had with him a familiar presence.

Azoz!

Seon wondered if they were hidden enough. Between the trees and the smoke, it seemed like the men with Azoz would not be able to see him. Emili was up in a tree, so she was not likely to be spotted. If she had a plan, she certainly wasn't letting Seon in on it.

The other question was how helpful Azoz would be. Normally, he would be an asset. He was much better in a fight than Seon. In this case though, he looked weak and disoriented. Seon wasn't sure reaching out to him would be the best idea either. He didn't know the abilities of the men with Azoz. It might give away Seon's position.

Azoz and his captor were followed by one last man, who seemed to have given up putting out the fire. All of them were running into the woods, with the man holding Azoz practically dragging him by the arm in his hurry. The last man joined him and grabbed Azoz's other arm to speed up the process.

They were coming closer. Apparently, the men had decided that rather than head the other way, they should go back through the woods toward town. And they were headed straight toward Seon and Emili. Emili was in a tree, well protected. There was no way they would not see Seon.

Go!

He was so focused on watching the men walking toward him that he almost didn't hear her. Of course, her voice was in his head so they didn't hear it. When it registered in his brain, he charged. By the time the men carrying Azoz had reached his tree, Seon was there.

Almost before he knew what was happening, Emili plunged down from the other side. She landed on top of one of the men, grabbing him around the neck and zapping him with a charge of electricity. Seon had seen Azoz do that, but never as powerfully. He pulled his knife from its sheath and stabbed the nearest man wildly, at the same time projecting a cloud of smoke into his senses and, hopefully, that of the others as well.

Seon was not sure if the smoke was working on all of the men, but it seemed to work on the one he was fighting. That man acted as if he couldn't see Seon or his captive. Taking advantage of the distraction, Seon grabbed a hold of Azoz's arm and propelled him backward, a clumsy move because at the same time he was grabbed from behind by one of Azoz's other captors.

The man who grabbed Seon did so wildly because he was having trouble seeing. Emili was fighting two men at the same time, though Seon was not sure how. He had his own problems. Fortunately, as weak as Azoz was, he managed to get up when Seon freed him. Since he was behind Seon, he stood up on wobbly feet and grabbed the closest thing he could reach, which turned out to be the back of the head of the man who was trying to strangle Seon.

That worked out well. As Seon struggled, he saw Azoz grab the man and cast volts of electricity into the back of his head with what little energy he had left. Then he collapsed backward and the men fell down on top of him. Seon stumbled, but was able to reach down and pull the man off of his fallen friend.

Meanwhile, Emili made short work of her two combatants. Seon didn't really see everything she did, but the two seemed to think that they could easily take on a lithe teenage girl. They were wrong. Emili made a gesture that looked like something Seon had seen at sporting events, starting with her palms facing opposite shoulders and then bringing them down in a slicing motion both ways across opposite sides of her chest. The look on her face was deadly.

The two men fell dead to the ground, and so did the trees behind them, sliced in half.

Emili turned to Seon. *Is he alright?*

I think so. Seon looked at Azoz, who was staring at Emili.

"Azoz, are you okay?" Seon said, panting to catch his breath.

"What?" Azoz looked startled. "Oh, right. Yeah. I think so. They drugged me with something, I guess."

His voice was a little slurred. Emili nodded and walked over to him. Before Seon could do anything, she was touching his shoulder and closing her eyes. He realized she was healing him, and much faster than anything Seon had ever done. She looked at him and he looked back at her. They must have communicated. Azoz nodded.

"Wow," Seon said.

"Yeah," Azoz agreed. "How about you? Are you alright?"

"Uh," Seon looked at the carnage around them. "Sure. I guess so. You are really going to have to tell us what happened.

"Not much to tell," Azoz shrugged. "I heard something, or sensed something. Then I went out into the forest. They got me."

"Try again," Seon said. Emili did not look like she was buying the story either.

Azoz grinned. "I was supposed to meet up with Corin. Obviously that didn't happen. I saw these suspicious looking guys outside of the village, and I followed them here. They grabbed me."

That sounded more like Azoz. Seon glared at him. He looked at Emili, but her expression was unreadable.

"Where's Corin?" Seon asked.

"I honestly don't know," Azoz said. "I'm supposed to meet him in Silvax."

"When?" Seon didn't like the sound of this. Emili was here, but now Corin wasn't, and they might still be in danger because the men they had just killed might need to report to someone.

"Tomorrow," Azoz said. "He'll know what to do about ... this." He gestured to the dead men.

No.

They both looked at Emili, who was giving Azoz a fiery look that made Seon glad it wasn't directed at him.

"Your idea?" Seon asked, speaking out loud for the benefit of Azoz, which he then realized was pointless because he must not be able to understand her.

Emili said nothing. She and Azoz continued to glare at each other. Seon sighed.

"Look, I'm glad you're okay, but this is all your fault," Seon said to Azoz. "Why did you leave me alone? If we are supposed to meet with Corin, why didn't we both go?"

"You assume too much," Azoz said flatly.

"That is not the point," Seon said. "You two dragged me here. To find her." He pointed to Emili. "You never told me why. She is in danger though. We are *all* in danger. Now we have to decide what to do."

"Fine," Azoz said. "What is your suggestion?"

"I don't have a suggestion," Seon said. "Except maybe, we listen to Emili."

They both looked expectantly at Emili.

Azoz nodded.

Seon looked at Emili expectantly. She raised her eyebrows. He could see her better now that during the fight her hood had fallen back. Her hair was flowing freely, and hung almost halfway down her back in rivulets. She was fierce and beautiful and positively furious.

Should we stay in the forest tonight? Seon asked her, deciding to go for the practical question first.

We need to take care of them first. She gestured to the bodies of the men they had faught. *You deal with them.* She pointed at Azoz. *This was your problem.*

Since Seon couldn't fault her thinking, he agreed with her. He gave Azoz a critical look and made a move toward the bodies. He was willing to help, but the question was how. If they were going to bury them, they would need a shovel. He didn't think they had anything like that in their gear.

Apparently they did. Azoz was opening his pack and removing some kind of tool. Emili was watching with a disinterested expression on her face. Seon went over to Azoz.

"Do I have one of those?" Seon asked.

"Yeah, you do. It unfolds and screws together," Azoz said, demonstrating with his.

Nodding, Seon opened his pack and looked through it until he found the tool. The pack definitely looked bigger on the inside than on the outside, and he was able to find the tool that Azoz was using. It unfolded and smoothed itself into a spade on one end, and there were pieces that screwed together to make a handle but it was still strong when he tried it in the dirt. The tool was clever, but seemed more mechanical than magical.

"It's enforced with a spell," Azoz said, as if reading his mind.

Seon nodded and the two of them got to work digging a pit. Although Seon had not bothered to wonder what Emili's contribution would be, he soon found out. She had a tiny flame going at the other end of the clearing and was soon cooking something in a small silver pot. Seon tried not to think about the proximity to the makeshift grave. He was getting much too comfortable with bodies of all kinds.

When they had a big enough hole, they rolled all six bodies into it. The hole was deep enough, because Azoz was strong and Seon was getting stronger by the day, but Seon still didn't like the idea of fighting and killing people and then just dumping their bodies in a hole. Once the hole was filled in, he dragged some fallen logs over it.

Emili? He had waited to ask her until she had finished cooking. *Can you do something with this? Make it look natural so no one knows what it is? I don't know, stone or something?*

Seon was not even sure what he was asking. He knew the bodies would decay and eventually become part of the ecosystem of the forest. His request was not so much about hiding them or honoring them, but about recognizing that they had once been human. Even if they were not good people when they died.

Emili must have understood. She walked over to the logs, and held out her hand, palm up. Closing her eyes, she held her hand out calmly and without moving it. Slowly, Seon and Azoz watched as the logs coalesced into one and then melted into stone. It wasn't any specific shape, but it was a marker that something was there, and something had happened.

Seon nodded. For the time and place, it was perfect. He looked at Azoz, whose face showed a mixture of surprise and respect. No one said anything, but they walked quietly over to the campfire and ate.

Chapter 22

After they had eaten, Seon found himself unsure what to do. He spoke to Emili with his mind, and Azoz with his voice. Emili and Azoz did not talk to each other at all. It made for some confusing conversations.

"Look, we are going to need to work together, for a while at least," Seon said. "I know that I do not speak the same language as Emili, but apparently you and Azoz can understand each other. I can understand Emili when she speaks to me. We can make this work."

Azoz looked up. "All we have to do is get to the village. I have a contact there."

I'm sure it will be that easy.

Seon looked at Emili, who was standing over by a tree. Her hood was back up, and due to the first signs of dusk he could not fully see the expression on her face. He could tell by her voice that she did not expect getting to the village to be as easy as Azoz was making it out to be.

"You don't have to tell me," Azoz said. "She disagrees."

"She does not think it will be easy," Seon said. "You can talk to her, can't you? Don't you speak her language?

Azoz shrugged, and Seon wasn't sure how to take that so he decided to drop it for the moment. He was not quite able to interpret what was going on between the two of them. Azoz seemed barely able to look at Emili, while she either ignored or scoffed at him.

"Okay, well, we can't do anything more tonight, but we can make a plan, right?" Seon said, looking at each of them, deciding from now on to try to think the exact same words after he said them for Emili.

Cooperation was not going to be easy with two people who wouldn't talk to each other.

I suppose the plan is to just walk into the village and knock on doors then? Sean asked her.

Emili did not take the bait. She gave Seon a stony look, and since he had not said the words out loud, Azoz did not know what he had said. Seon didn't bother repeating it. This was getting them nowhere. He tried a different tactic.

"Who is your contact?" Seon asked Azoz.

"Does it matter?" Azoz opened his pack and removed a bedroll and then stretched out with his head on it, even though the sun was barely setting. "I am the only one he will talk to."

"Don't you think you should tell us what we are getting into?" Seon said, frowning.

He realized that Azoz had been through a lot that day and was probably tired. He had been kidnapped, drugged, and in a fight. Meeting Emili was probably emotional too, since he had been tasked to look for her. Seon thought there might be something more to that as well, but tried not to overcomplicate things. He did not want to worry about Azoz's feelings or lack of feelings for Emili.

"It won't matter," Azoz repeated. "You can't go into the village without me."

"And what happens if we get separated again?" Seon said. "I have to know where I am supposed to meet, or who I am supposed to meet. If Emili is supposed to be somewhere, she deserves to know. She deserves to choose. Maybe she doesn't want to go."

Azoz glared at that last comment. Since the beginning, the

mission had been to find Emili and bring her somewhere, but Seon did not know where. There had never been any question of giving her a choice.

Now Emili was no longer a vision in a dream. She was a real person to Seon. She was no helpless damsel in distress either. As far as Seon was concerned, as capable as Azoz was, she was stronger and more dangerous than both of them put together. They were not going to take her anywhere. If she went, it was because she wanted to go.

"Does she?" Azoz asked.

They both looked at Emili. She was no longer leaning against the tree. Now she was sitting at the base of it, cross-legged. Her hood was still up, so they could barely see her face. Seon thought she looked mysterious that way. He had no idea what she was thinking.

I think he has no plan.

Seon had to agree. Azoz either had no plan or was choosing to withhold it. Either was reckless. He turned to Azoz.

"She says you have no plan," Seon told him.

Azoz treated Emili to his signature smirk. "She doesn't need to know my plan."

Apparently that needed no translation. Even from under the hood, Seon could see the snap of the fire in Emili's purpley eyes. She was not amused.

"I think there has to be a compromise," Seon said. "Even if we do not want to give everyone all of the plan, because we do not all trust one another, surely we can decide on a plan where each person has a part." He added Emili's thought for her benefit.

"Such as?" Azoz asked.

"I don't know," Seon said. "Maybe you could go in first, make contact, and then we will meet you."

"No," Azoz said."

"Why not?" Seon asked.

"I just don't think we should be separated again," Azoz said.

"Whose fault was it that we were separated last time?" Seon asked.

At an impasse, the two stared at one another. Seon was keenly aware that Emili was watching them and felt a little sheepish about it. He had argued with Azoz plenty of times before, but never with an audience.

Do you have a suggestion? Seon asked her.

You two go. I will remain here. Emili said.

Seon looked at Azoz, trying to decide how, or if, to convey that suggestion. Azoz was not going to like this one bit. He looked at Emili, and then at Azoz.

"She says she will wait here, and then we will go into the village," Seon said.

"No."

Whatever response he had expected, an unemotional flat 'no,' had not been it. Maybe Azoz had been expecting that suggestion. He didn't even consider it or counter it. He didn't seem angry at Emili either. Seon couldn't read him at all.

Seon turned to Emili. *That doesn't require translation.*

No. It doesn't. But that is what we will do. I will stay at the edge of the forest. You two will identify the contact and make sure he is there. When you have done so, you will signal me. Her eyes flashed at Azoz under her hood. *Tell him.*

Seon sighed, and then repeated the message to Azoz. He listened without a word. Seon knew that while he didn't like it, there was little Azoz could do. They couldn't force Emili to come with them. Unless one of them had a better plan and got her to agree to it, they might as well go along with hers.

"I think she's right," Seon said. "We have to make sure your contact is there. If you want, I can stay here until you check."

Azoz shook his head. "No, you are better off with me. Then you will know who the contact is, hopefully, if something happens to me."

Now that they finally had a plan, Seon realized he was exhausted. He retrieved his bedroll and stretched out. Emili remained in the same position, although her eyes were closed. She seemed to be meditating. Seon hoped she got some rest as he drifted off to sleep.

When he opened his eyes the next morning, neither Azoz nor Emili were anywhere to be seen. Almost out of habit, Seon closed his eyes and reached out with his senses. Luckily, they were both nearby. Since he decided that neither were in danger, he stayed where he was, reached into his pack, and ate some dried berries. In a few minutes, Azoz returned with some kind of small fowl. Alix was flying low over his head.

"Where's Emili?" Seon asked.

"Shouldn't I be asking you that?" Azoz asked.

Seon thought there was a little too much venom in that retort for a joke. He eyed Azoz carefully as Alix landed on a log next to him and started preening her feathers.

"Why is that?" Seon asked.

"Oh, I don't know," Azoz said. "You two seem awfully cozy."

"I barely know her, Azoz," Seon said. "You're the one who acts all strange around her."

"Strange!" Azoz said. "The way you look at her?"

"How? How do I look at her?" Seon was on his feet before he even realized it.

Then he stopped, wondering if his defensiveness meant that Azoz was onto something. He did feel a connection to Emili, but it was not the kind that Azoz was implying. At least he didn't think it was. She was beautiful and exotic and he loved looking at her, but he barely knew her and he wasn't the type to fall for a girl just because he met her in a dream.

"What difference does it make?" Seon added. "She will go off somewhere, and I will likely never see her again."

"How do you know what?" Azoz asked. "What makes you think that you will never see her again. Where will she be going? Where will you be going?

At this question, Seon realized he did not know. Corin had said something about finding someone to train him, and Azoz had been to an academy, but Seon did not know where it was. Seon began to wonder if he and Emili might end up in the same place after all. He realized he had been preparing himself to only know her for a short time, when he wanted to get to know her better. He might get a chance to get to know her better.

"Exactly," Azoz said.

Seon did not like Azoz's smug tone. The entire conversation was frustrating and confusing to him, just as most of the time when he was given only bits of the information. He didn't know anything about this world he had only just started to be a part of and every time he learned something, it was like only getting a small peek, peeling a corner back of the curtain of the window. Seon wanted to know more, but he wasn't going to get it from Azoz, at least not right now.

Azoz sat down and cleaned his fowl, and was cooking it over a small fire when Emili returned. She had been gathering berries, and shared a few from a small sack of them with Seon and Azoz. They were good—about the size of a thumb, yellow and sour-sweet. Azoz offered Emili a small portion of his fowl and, to Seon's surprise, she took it.

"Do you have any kind of signal worked out?" Seon asked.

"Actually yes," Azoz said. "It's a pub. We go in and order a specific drink, and they will know it's me."

"Really?" Seon said.

"Really," Azoz said. "It's not on the menu. It's just a signal."

All in all, that seemed reasonable. The three of them packed up, made sure to clear the camp completely, and then walked to the edge of the forest. Emili stayed hidden and Seon and Azoz walked through the woods. They left their packs hidden, but they were still armed.

Seon felt strange and exposed being in a civilization area again. Fortunately, he and Azoz were dressed in a manner close enough to the local citizenry that they did not stand out. It was not a prosperous village, and most of the people wore clothing in worse shape than theirs was in.

As expected, it was difficult to do reconnaissance in a small village. They did not go to the pub first thing. Instead, they went to a vendor and bought some fruit rolls. They were a type of pastry made of fruit, bread, and cream. After eating nothing but berries and forage for days, Seon found the baked goods heavenly.

They found an alley that had access to a rooftop with a good view of the pub, and watched it for several hours. At first, no one went in or out. Around the midday meal, the pub got more business but it was never very busy. Once Azoz was satisfied that the clientele was safe and no one was watching the building, they hopped down and walked the back way around into the pub.

The place did not look like anywhere Seon would order something meant to consume. It was dark, dusty, and smelled of mold and possibly urine. In a corner booth there was a large hairy man who was asleep and snoring, but he was the only customer at the time. Azoz walked up to the bar as if he had done it a dozen times and placed his order in an undertone.

Seon didn't hear what he ordered, but apparently the woman behind the counter did. She was barely tall enough to see over it, and almost as wide as she was tall. Her hair was bright white and she was wearing a dirty apron that might have once been white over a shift whose color Seon could only guess at. When she opened her mouth to smirk at them, she seemed to have few teeth. She said nothing, but disappeared.

She made Seon nervous. The pub made Seon nervous. It was like something out of a bad mystery novel. He was sure she was going to go into the back and give them up. Instead, she returned with a tall, narrow glass filled with a fluorescent turquoise liquid specked with gold.

Azoz dropped a coin on the counter, took the drink, and went to the booth in the opposite corner from the snoring giant. Seon sat down across from him and gave him a pointed look. He was doubting Azoz was going to drink the horrifying concoction. Seon definitely wasn't going to. He had never tried alcohol before except once when his brother once gave him some ale on a dare. A strange pub like this was not the place to do it.

As far as Seon was concerned, this was the worst part. They were supposed to wait for their contact. Anyone could just as easily betray them now.

For one thing, Seon did not like Azoz's choice of tables. He felt trapped. They could see the doors, and no one could sneak up on them, but they could not get out either. It had advantages and disadvantages, he had to admit. There had been no way to scout the pub from the inside.

Seon knew that Azoz was the expert here. He was the one with the training, and Seon was just second-guessing him and nervous because they were sitting, waiting. Not knowing what to do was making Seon more frightened and agitated. Maybe he should have tried the beverage, to calm his nerves.

After what seemed like years, but was really only a little over an hour, the back door to the pub opened. Both Seon and Azoz had been pretending to play a game using small polished stones that Seon knew nothing about. Anyone who looked closely would have realized they were not really playing. Neither looked up when the door opened, and Seon worked hard not to betray that he noticed. His nerves felt like frayed wires.

As Seon picked up one of his stones, pretending to make a move, he listened to soft footsteps moving across the room to their table. He did not look up until the person sat down next to Azoz. Seon put down his stone. Azoz said something, and the person said something in return. It was a woman's voice.

Chapter 23

"Let's go."

The words were whispered so quietly that Seon barely heard Azoz say them. He followed him and the woman outside of the pub through the back door. No one said a word.

As they walked through the alleys of the village, Seon could barely see the woman. She was not much taller than he was, and dressed in a plain brown dress of some kind of coarse material with a shawl over her head and shoulders that was woven with many colors. She wore boots similar to theirs, and she was walking very quickly.

The woman ducked from one alley into another and then finally into a doorway for what was barely more than a hovel. It was almost as dark as the pub, but she lit what looked like an oil lamp when they got inside. Seon realized the place had only one window, and it was covered with a heavy cloth. The place had only one room, with a bed, a table with three chairs, a strange looking stove, and what was probably a sink.

When she lit the lamp and removed her shawl, Seon saw that she was younger than he had thought, not much older than them, and quite pretty. Her hair was yellow and her face was round with big gray eyes. She gave them a serious look, and then a smile, and then said something to Azoz.

"She says she doesn't think we were followed," Azoz said.

"That's good," Seon said.

"Her name is Ava," Azoz said. "She is our contact, obviously. She has not seen Corin. She says we will stay here until he comes."

"Wait, what?" Seon said. "Here? You agreed to this."

"Just for now," Azoz said. "It's a safehouse."

"Oh," Seon said, looking around. "It's safe ... uh, secure?"

"Hopefully," Azoz said.

"Sure," Seon said. "Thank her for me, okay. The Umbra ... are they here?"

"I asked her that," Azoz said. "Or, I asked her if she knows who the Umbra agents are. There are agents of course, but they come and go, so it's not always clear who they are."

"Great," Seon said. "How do you say thank you?"

"*Grati*," Azoz said.

Seon turned to Ava. "Grati."

Ava smiled and made a little gesture almost like a bow, and then left. Seon watched her go, and then walked over to the table and sat down heavily. He looked at Azoz.

"Is Corin going to do the same thing we did? Come into the pub and order the drink and meet Ava and come here?" Seon asked.

"No, of course not," Azoz said. "Corin will find us though. He will find me."

"Of course. You are not honestly suggesting that we just stay here, are you?" Seon said.

The whole idea sounded ridiculous. While Seon had not necessarily felt safe at many points during this journey, here, in this 'safe house' he felt the least safe of all. While it sounded grand to be in a village where there were real beds and food vendors, there were also Umbra agents. Seon could not think of any place he wanted to be less.

"Look, Seon, I know you are uncomfortable, but there aren't people jumping out to get you behind every corner," Azoz said.

"Are you sure?" Seon asked.

"I'm sure," Azoz said. "We need to be cautious, but remember that while they are looking for us, they also have to find us."

Seon felt that comment was typically cryptic of Azoz and did not appreciate it.

"When are we going to signal Emili?" Seon asked.

"There's time enough for that," Azoz said. "Corin is not here yet."

"So we stay here and enjoy ourselves and wait for Corin?" Seon said.

"You make it sound like that is a bad thing," Azoz said.

"It does not look very good, no," Seon said. "Emili is waiting for us to signal her."

"We will, once Corin is here," Azoz said.

"That was not the agreement," Seon said.

"I don't think it was that specific," Azoz said.

The two of them glared at each other.

"What would you have us do? Just you and me?" Azoz asked.

"I don't know," Seon said. "But tell me this. When Corin does find us, what happens then? After Emili is with us. Where are we going?"

"What do you mean?" Azoz asked.

Seon thought that Azoz was being evasive.

"You said that I was acting like I would never see Emili again," Seon said. "Where are we going? Is a spaceship going to land in the middle of town and take the four of us away?"

"Don't be ridiculous," Azoz said.

"Why not?" Seon said. "I have seen any number of things in the past few days that I would have said were impossible before. Who's to say that is not possible? Does Corin have a spaceship? Do you know what a spaceship is?"

"I know what a spaceship is," Azoz said. "Corin does not have one. That is part of your world, not mine, and from what I can tell, your kind do not use them for much."

"You're right, we don't," Seon said. "But as for as I know, your kind might."

"Okay, you have me there," Azoz said. "But we don't."

"You have portals," Seon said.

"A portal is not the same thing as a spaceship," Azoz said.

"No, Seon said, "I guess it is not. Will we take a portable portal?"

Azoz sighed. "You ask too many questions. Why would we have taken the journey on foot if we could have gotten there that quickly?"

"Why indeed?" Seon asked pointedly.

Instead of responding, Azoz stood up and walked over to the window. He removed the heavy window covering from the corner and peaked out. Then he let it drop. A puff of dust wafted up after it.

"I think we can get some food, but only one of us should go," Azoz said. "Do you want me to do it?"

"Do I trust you, you mean?" Seon asked. "I think we should go together."

"No," Azoz said.

"Let's see if there's food here," Seon said.

They searched the hovel, and found a basket under a cloth with fresh bread, some salted meat, and dried berries. It wasn't much, but obviously Ava had stocked the safe house with provisions. Seon was grateful to her, and wondered if Azoz felt bad for wanting to go out.

After they ate, they rested for a few hours. Seon meditated and reached out to see that Emili was comfortable and waiting for them. He told her that they were safe, but that Corin was not with them. It was frustrating to wait, but Seon had to agree that there were few other options. He kept the contact short, in case someone overheard it. It was a risk they would have to take.

When night fell, Seon and Azoz were both restless. They had figured that if Corin came, it would be then, but Azoz had not had any contact. Although he hadn't said anything, Seon could tell that Azoz was worried. It was an unusual look for him.

Azoz was sitting on the floor against the wall that faced the alley with his crystal in his hand. Seon watched him try to reach out for his mentor. He was nervous for Azoz, and for himself. He had tried searching for Corin as well, but he didn't have Azoz's connection.

After a few hours of this, Azoz gave a start.

"He's here," Azoz said, his voice a near whisper. "But something's wrong."

"What is it?" Seon asked.

"I don't know," Azoz said.

His voice was strained, and Seon could tell he was worried. Azoz jumped up, and moved toward the door. Seon moved to intercept him.

"You're going out there?" Seon asked.

"I have to," Azoz said.

"What if it's a trap?" Seon asked.

"It doesn't matter," Azoz said. "Corin is here, and he didn't say *not* to come."

"He didn't tell you to come either," Seon said. "If there is a problem, should we get Emili?"

"No!" Azoz said.

"She's better in a fight than either of us," Seon said. "She'll probably know there's trouble anyway."

"How?" Azoz asked. "Did you tell her?"

"No," Seon said. "But I think we should."

Before Azoz could answer or change his mind, Seon was leaning against the wall and reaching out to Emili. Azoz apparently decided to let him be. There wasn't much he could do to stop it.

Emili, can you hear me? We need you. Something is happening. They're here.

Although he could not clearly tell her response, he knew that she heard him and she was coming. That was enough for Seon. He opened his eyes and looked at Azoz, who was still clutching his own crystal and reaching out to try to find Corin.

It took some time for Azoz to find Corin, and Seon could tell when he did. His head snapped up, and then he went to the door. Seon and Azoz exchanged glances, confirming that they were ready.

"Do you know where to go?" Seon asked.

Azoz nodded, "Let's go."

Azoz opened the door, and they slunk out of it into the cool dark night. The alley was empty, and so were the streets beyond. Seon followed Azoz, who seemed to know what direction he was headed. Seon had his knife in his hand. He reached out with his senses for people, but also wild dogs or any other animals that might be helpful. Sometimes he wished he had Azoz's more direct skills and could just shoot bolts of electricity into his enemies.

It turned out they were headed for the outskirts of town. Azoz slowed down, and then stopped. Seon asked him a question with a look, although it was so dark that he wasn't sure if Azoz saw it.

"Something's here," Seon said softly, sensing danger nearby.

He barely had time to get the words out before there was a flash up ahead. Azoz ran toward it. Seon's instinct was to run the other way, but he followed, staying close to the buildings. The flash reminded him of the alley back home, when Azoz had been injured. That attack seemed like a lifetime ago.

Fortunately, Seon had learned a few things since then. He kept a low profile and reached out with his senses. A few streets away there was some kind of medium sized street animal roaming, and Seon used it as a distraction by leading it toward the commotion. It worked, because Seon heard a roar and a hiss only a moment or two later as the animal startled the combatants.

Emili was nearby. She was either above them or ahead of them. Seon could not tell. He had no idea where Corin was. There were at least three other men, so Seon tried to get into the fray as quickly as he could, so as not to leave Azoz to face them by himself.

It being dark was not helpful. They hadn't spent enough time in the village earlier for Seon to get to know the terrain, and it was harder to get a feel for the place than it was in a forest where he could feel the plants and animals around him. He could tell that there were some people in the surrounding buildings, but they were no threat. Most of them were either afraid or indifferent. Seon felt sorry for the ones who were afraid and grateful for the ones who were indifferent. It was better that no one else tried to interfere.

Someone tried to grab Seon from behind, and he reacted by instinct, ducking and kicking out with his foot while strafing with the knife as forcefully as he could at the same time. Both moves were mostly distraction as he used his real defense, which was to try to enhance the darkness in his attacker's vision. It was dark enough outside, but Seon tried to play up that darkness to make it seem pitch black.

His assailant stumbled, confused. Seon took advantage of that momentum to knock him down. He was struggling to get the drop on him when the guy grabbed Seon's arm and tried to pull him down. Then he just stopped moving when someone snapped his neck from behind.

Emili had arrived.

Chapter 24

Emili favored him with a brief smile and then hopped back toward the fray. Seon looked up. There was definitely mayhem there. He followed her, hoping that he would be more of a help than a hindrance. Then he almost tripped on some type of weapon.

The man he had been fighting with must have dropped it, and Seon was glad he hadn't been on the receiving end. This must have been what they were shooting with. Even though Seon had no idea how to use it, he picked it up. Emili must have seen no use for it. She didn't seem to need a gun. She was a walking weapon.

Seon ran after Emili, who hopped on top of the roof of a two story building in one jump. Since he could not follow her there easily, he ran along the street and tried to follow the fight. He could see flashes of light up ahead and knew it had moved there. Azoz and Corin were struggling against three of the Umbra, dressed in the same black shiny leather as the men they had fought before back in Seon's city.

This was when Seon realized the disadvantage of a gun, especially when he had no training in how to use the weapon. If he simply aimed it and shot into the fray, he was just as likely to hit friend as foe. Seon decided to save the weapon for when someone was running at him. He leaned against the building, trying to calculate the best way he could help.

Emili seemed to be making her own calculations. As Azoz and Corin were struggling three against two, she catapulted herself off the rooftop, down on top of the third man, who was not expecting a girl to jump from a two story building down directly onto him. Seon took that opportunity to dive in and grab one of the other two from the back, knock him to the ground, and shoot him.

At point-blank range the weapon wasn't difficult to aim. The problem was that it didn't shoot bullets like a gun. Instead, it shot rays of electricity. The power was more than Seon expected, and the recoil sent him reeling backward. He managed to stay on his feet, but only barely.

There was only one man left, and Corin made short work of him by blasting him into the side of a building using telekinetic force. Emili, Azoz, and Corin dragged the bodies into an alley and piled them behind a trash receptacle. No one said a word. It was pitch black in the alley, but Corin had produced a small light from somewhere.

That done, they returned to the safe house to rest and take stock of injuries. Azoz and Corin were both injured, but Azoz's injuries were worse. Emili sat in a corner of the bed curled up in her cloak with her hood up while Seon attended to Azoz's injuries. Seon was exhausted, but was hoping that he was strong enough to heal both of them.

"Seon."

Seon looked up. Corin was standing over him. He must have either passed out or fallen asleep.

"I'm sorry, Sir," Seon said groggily. "Are you alright? Do you need help? Is Emili hurt?"

Corin shook his head. "Emili is fine. She healed my injuries. You have done well. Azoz is healed. Get some rest."

Seon could feel himself nodding. He felt himself falling asleep. He was glad to know everyone was okay.

When he woke up again, it was morning. Azoz, Corin and, surprisingly, Emili, were sitting at the little table. Someone had brought food from the village. There was a basket of fruit rolls as well as another one of what looked like local fresh fruit. It all smelled wonderful to Seon, who was suddenly ravenous.

"Hey," Azoz said cheerfully. "Look who's awake."

"Ugh," Seon said. "Food."

"Help yourself," Azoz said, tossing a round blue fruit the size of a closed fist at Seon.

Seon caught it, and felt the skin experimentally.

"You peel it," Corin suggested.

Seon nodded, and did so. The fruit had a fingernail-thick skin, but it was easy to peel. Inside were slices of juicy red fruit that was so moist he had to catch it with his hand to keep from dribbling it everywhere. It was delicious.

After eating the fruit, Seon joined Corin and Azoz at the table for the bread rolls and sampled some other local fruits and nuts. There wasn't much conversation, but the atmosphere was calmer and freer than Seon had felt with any of them. Even Emili seemed more relaxed. She was once again cuddled up in a corner of the bed wrapped in her shawl.

Perhaps the threat of imminent death is behind us, at least for now. Seon thought.

"After we eat, we are going to go back to the forest to get your packs, and then we are leaving," Corin said.

"That's it?" Seon said. "Where are we going?"

"We are leaving," Corin said, "because we have done what we came to do."

"Are we walking back?" Seon asked. "Because it took awhile to get here."

"It did," Corin said, "but we are not going back to where we came from."

Seon thought about that. That did make sense. He remembered the question he had asked before, as well as the answer, and decided it was better not to ask.

"Right," Seon said. "So we are going ahead?"

"Exactly," Corin said. "It is always best to move forward."

The End

www.ingramcontent.com/pod-product-compliance
Lightning Source LLC
Chambersburg PA
CBHW070451120726
47910CB00003B/1005